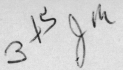 

"I don't think you saw a body being dumped."

"If it wasn't a body, then what? Drugs? Weapons?"

The woman wasn't going to relent, was she? "The Colombian drug cartel has a pipeline to the U.S. through the Keys. Arms dealers are a dime a dozen, especially around the Gulf of Mexico."

Detective Angie Carlucci peered at him with suspicion in her eyes. "You're not a simple boat captain. Who are you?"

For her own good, he couldn't reveal his identity. If she kept pushing, she'd find out how dangerous things could get. "Trust me, you'll be safer if you pretend you didn't see anything."

"No can do. I've sworn an oath to uphold the law."

Jason shook his head with exasperation and admiration. The woman was a spitfire determined to do the right thing. He couldn't blame her. But she had no idea what kind of hornet's nest she'd stumbled into.

That meant it was up to Jason to keep Detective Carlucci safe.

Books by Terri Reed

Love Inspired Suspense

Strictly Confidential
*Double Deception
Beloved Enemy
Her Christmas Protector
*Double Jeopardy
*Double Cross
*Double Threat Christmas
Her Last Chance
Chasing Shadows
Covert Pursuit

*The McClains

Love Inspired

Love Comes Home
A Sheltering Love
A Sheltering Heart
A Time of Hope
Giving Thanks for Baby

TERRI REED

At an early age Terri Reed discovered the wonderful world of fiction and declared she would one day write a book. Now she is fulfilling that dream and enjoys writing for Steeple Hill. Her second book, *A Sheltering Love,* was a 2006 RITA® Award Finalist and a 2005 National Readers' Choice Award Finalist. Her book *Strictly Confidential,* book five of the Faith at the Crossroads continuity series, took third place in the 2007 American Christian Fiction Writers Book of the Year Award, and *Her Christmas Protector* took third place in 2008. She is an active member of both Romance Writers of America and American Christian Fiction Writers. She resides in the Pacific Northwest with her college-sweetheart husband, two wonderful children and an array of critters. When not writing, she enjoys spending time with her family and friends, gardening and playing with her dogs.

You can write to Terri at P.O. Box 19555, Portland, OR 97280. Visit her on the Web at www.loveinspiredauthors.com, leave comments on her blog at www.ladiesofsuspense.blogspot.com or e-mail her at terrireed@sterling.net.

COVERT PURSUIT

Terri Reed

Steeple
Hill®

Published by Steeple Hill Books™

STEEPLE HILL BOOKS

Steeple
Hill®

Recycling programs
for this product may
not exist in your area.

ISBN-13: 978-0-373-44392-5

COVERT PURSUIT

www.SteepleHill.com

Printed in U.S.A.

They shall call my name, and I will hear them;
I will say, it is my people; and they shall say,
The Lord is my God.
—*Zechariah* 13:9

Though writing is a solitary endeavor nothing is done in a vacuum. Thank you Leah, Lissa and Ruth for walking through this with me. Thank you to my editors Emily Rodmell and Tina James for believing in this story and in me.

PROLOGUE

January

"Agent down!" Immigration and Customs Enforcement Special Agent Jason Buchett yelled as he scrambled on hands and knees across the hard-packed earth of the New Mexico desert to reach his fellow agent and best friend, Garrett Smyth.

The light of the full moon revealed blood gushing from a neck wound just above the flak vest guarding Garrett's chest. The well-aimed shot was meant to inflict both pain and death. A fact pounding through Jason's horrified mind as he applied pressure to the wound. Sticky, warm liquid oozed between his fingers.

All around them the exchange of gunfire rang in the night air, friendly fire from the agents advancing and enemy fire from Picard's men coming from the windows and recesses of the large villa outlined by the moon's glow.

Jason and Garrett were part of the team sent in to raid the elusive illegal arms dealer's fortress.

And they'd been expected.

The latest intel suggested that their primary target wasn't even there. This had all been for nothing.

"Come on, Garrett, don't do this to me. You gotta hang on!"

Garrett's tanned, hard-lined face showed pain but he managed a weak smile. "Yeah, make it about you."

"Not today, brother. Today it's about you living. You have to live!"

Jason's heart twisted. Terror throbbed in his veins. He couldn't lose his friend.

Please, Lord, spare him. I'll do anything, anything You ask!

Garrett had been Jason's anchor during the rough years of his mother's illness and death. And after Serena had broken off their engagement, Garrett had pulled Jason out of the bottle, effectively saving not only his career, but his life.

The light in Garrett's blue eyes dimmed, sending fresh panic and despair roaring over Jason. "Garrett!"

"Keep up the good fight," Garrett said, his voice warbled. "I'll see you in Heaven."

"Garrett, don't you die!"

Garrett's eyes closed and his body seemed to sigh as he went limp in Jason's arms. Death claimed him.

Jason hung his head. Tears of sorrow and rage gathered in his eyes. The burn of a building roar of anguish tore through his chest. Ignoring the risk to his own life, he threw back his head and let loose an agonizing sound until his dry throat hurt.

In a voice filled with determination and fire, he vowed, "No matter how long it takes or what it costs, I will bring down Felix Picard!"

The only trouble was he didn't have an ID on Picard.

He had absolutely nothing.

ONE

June

The setting sun decorated the sky over the ocean with streaks of red, gold and hints of the midnight that would soon overtake the perfect powder-blue of a summer day in Florida. Light bounced off the waters of the Gulf of Mexico and bathed Homicide Detective Angie Carlucci's restless nature in soothing warmth. She didn't mind the humidity she'd been warned about.

Staring out at the serene horizon, she searched for signs of the brewing storm the weatherman had predicted. There were none that she could see.

Sitting on the deck of her aunt's vacation cottage a stone's throw from the shelled beach of Loribel Island, she tried to unwind against the cushioned backrest of a wooden Adirondack chair and propped her feet on the railing. Inactivity made her antsy.

There wasn't even a television to veg out in front

of. And no cable even if she wanted to buy a TV. She'd already tried going online. But noooo. No Internet. Not even a wireless connection she could piggyback on. At least her cell phone picked up a random signal now and again. The roaming charges were going to be murder on her phone bill.

She let out a long-suffering sigh and wiggled her red-tipped toenails, the result of her mother's insistence she have a spa day before leaving Boston on vacation.

Angie had to admit she rather liked the way the polish made her feet look. Small and dainty. So unlike how she normally felt.

Bored, she closed her eyes and breathed in deeply of the fresh salty air, tasting the brine of the ocean, savoring the feel of moisture and heat on her skin.

Come on, relax.

The problem was she didn't see any purpose in a vacation. So she worked more hours than needed, so she didn't have a social life to speak of, that didn't mean she wasn't content with her life. It was everyone around her who thought she needed to take time off.

Rest, everyone kept saying. She slept most nights just fine, thank you very much.

In the distance she heard the rumble of a motorboat. She'd watched so many boats coming and going from the marina a mile or so down the beach that she could almost picture the vessel in her head: sleek, fast and luxurious. Seemed everyone on the island had a boat of some sort.

Maybe tomorrow she'd rent one. That would be fun. And active. Something sleek and fast. Yeah, real fast.

She realized she wasn't the sit-on-the-beach-and-do-nothing sort of vacationer even if she wanted to be.

The noise of the motor cut off abruptly. Angie opened her eyes. Sure enough, a slick, white twenty-five-foot craft with lots of chrome railings bobbed in the water at least a hundred yards offshore. Two white males heaved something long and black over the side of the boat.

Angie's feet dropped to the deck and her heart rate kicked into high gear.

A body bag.

Those men just dumped a body into the ocean!

The engine restarted and the boat sped off.

She jumped to her feet and ran for her cell phone, praying she'd have a strong enough signal to dial 911. She did. She quickly identified herself and explained the situation. The operator put her on hold.

"Seriously?" Angie said to the silent line.

Every instinct in her screamed for action. While keeping the phone cradled between her ear and her shoulder, she searched for her shoes. She crouched down to find one slip-on sneaker under the sofa. The other she found near the stairs leading to the loft bedroom.

From the drawer in the kitchen, she snatched her compact Glock, kangaroo holster and badge before grabbing the keys to her rental car. She left the cottage and drove in her rented convertible toward the marina. She was sure she'd recognize the boat if she saw it again.

Finally, the operator returned to the line.

"The chief's on his way."

"Tell him to meet me at the marina on the south side of the island."

Angie hung up and concentrated on not speeding through the peaceful streets populated with cyclists and pedestrians of all sorts.

Feeling alive for the first time since she'd arrived on the island, Angie savored the rush of adrenaline pumping through her veins. This was what God meant for her to be: protector of the innocent, the righter of wrongs, the one who brought the bad guys to justice and gave the families of the dead peace.

The image of the body bag played across her mind.

Whoever was now at the bottom of the ocean deserved her attention.

She found a parking place in the small lot, then ran to the docks, her gaze seeking out the boat she'd seen. The sun had completely set, but thankfully the tall, high-powered overhead lights provided plenty of illumination as she ran from one end of the dock to the other, searching for the vessel.

Frustration beat an uneven rhythm at her temple. The slick white boat wasn't moored anywhere.

The sudden sensation of being watched raised the fine hairs at the back of her neck. She jerked to a stop and slowly scanned the area for danger. Her gaze landed on a six-foot-two, mid-thirties white male, only a few feet away. He was wiping down the sides of his expensive boat. Curiosity etched in the lines of his strikingly handsome face and radiated from his blue eyes.

It probably wasn't every day he saw a woman running up and down the marina like a crazy person.

Tall, lean and unmistakably well muscled beneath a bright yellow polo shirt and ridiculously loud Bermuda shorts, he looked the quintessential yachtsman. His light brown hair was longer in the front and flopped attractively over his forehead.

Angie arched one eyebrow as a means to deter additional interest. To her chagrin, he smiled. A slow, awareness-grabbing smile that squeezed the air from her lungs.

The screech of tires broke through her momentary daze and made her snap to attention. Dismissing the too-handsome man as any sort of threat, she watched a forest-green truck with a light bar across the cab's roof and the official Loribel Island Police Department decal on the door jerk to a halt at the pathway leading from the parking lot to the docks. An older, silver-haired man stepped out and hurried down the path to her.

Angie turned her back on the good-looking boater to focus on Loribel Island's chief of police. She stuck out her hand. "Chief…?"

"Chief Decker." He shook her hand. "You the one who called in a dead body?"

"Detective Angie Carlucci, Boston P.D.," she said, and then explained the situation.

Decker frowned. "So you didn't actually see the body?"

"I saw a body bag. If you have access to a boat I can take you to where I witnessed the dump. It was approximately a hundred yards from shore."

"You're staying at Teresa Gambini's place, right?" Stroking his chin, Decker glanced at the nearly dark sky. "Well, now, by the time I get one of our boats from the other end of the island it'll be pitch-black out on the water. Even the coast guard wouldn't be able to get a boat out here any sooner."

"And in the meantime the tide carries the body away," Angie stated as disbelief at the man's lack of concern and urgency poured through her.

"That's certainly a possibility. We'll make a wide search of the area. If there is a dead body, there's nothing we can do for the person now. The morning will be soon enough."

Deep down she agreed, dusk was rapidly closing in, but it still galled her to wait. "What time tomorrow?"

Decker shrugged. "Nine, tenish."

"Great. I'll be here at nine," she said, irritated by his lackadaisical attitude. "In the meantime, you could have the other marina checked for the boat I saw."

He gave her a patient smile, showing aged and crooked teeth. "Yes, ma'am, I could do that." He took a small notepad from the breast pocket of his green uniform. "Details?"

She described the boat. "It had three words written across the side, but I think they were in a foreign language."

"That's not much to go on. A lot of boats fit that description. If I have any questions, how can I reach you?"

She rattled off her cell-phone number. "But I'll see you in the morning."

Decker eyed her a long moment. "I think, Detective Carlucci, you should enjoy your vacation on the island and leave the police work to us. If I have anything to tell you, I'll call."

With that he walked back to his truck and drove away. Angie stared after him.

"Well, that was awfully condescending of him," a Southern-accented male voice said behind her.

She whirled around to find herself staring into the smoky-blue eyes of the yachtsman. Up close he was even more appealing. Firm features with strength of character etched in the straight line of his jaw and a confident set to his wide shoulders. Some elemental warning alerted her senses.

She shouldn't be noticing his attractiveness, not when he'd been able to move so close without her knowledge. Usually her senses were sharper, more acute to potential danger.

The tranquility of the island must have dulled her wits, she rationalized and frowned with wariness.

She backed up a step, creating more space between them. "Do you normally eavesdrop on other people's conversations?"

"Only when they're two feet away and aren't exactly keeping their voices low," he said in a tone as smooth as Earl Grey on a brisk New England morning.

Unexpected little shivers traipsed over her skin. She rubbed her arms and conceded his point with a nod. "Right. Excuse me."

She turned to leave. His hand shot out and clasped her right elbow in a tight grip. Alarm flushed through her system. Her heart rammed against her rib cage in a painful cadence. Instinct took over.

She pivoted right, wrenching her elbow back and away as her stiff left hand thumped hard against his forearm, effectively breaking his hold. Once free, she jumped back to land in a fighter's stance, weight on right leg, left leg ready to kick if need be. Her right hand gripped the butt of her holstered weapon.

She'd been wrong. The man posed a threat. She just didn't know how much of one. Or why.

Surprise washed over the guy's face. He jerked his hands up in a show of entreaty, palms out, fingers splayed. "Whoa, whoa! Hey, Detective, I didn't mean any harm."

"Don't move."

"Wouldn't dream of it," he drawled in his thick Southern accent.

"Who are you? And what do you want?"

"Name's Jason Bodewell." He gestured toward the classy boat behind him. "I charter my boat out for the tourist trade."

Taking calming breaths, Angie relaxed her stance slightly. "Okay. So…?"

One side of his well-formed mouth lifted. "So, I was going to offer to take you out."

She blinked. Heat crept up her neck. *What?* "Out?"

His eyebrows rose. "To look for the body."

A little embarrassed groan escaped. "Oh. Right." So he'd heard everything. What was he? Some sort of crime-scene gawker? Or just a good citizen wanting to help?

Though her heart rate beat faster than normal, the adrenaline eased. She moved her hand away from her Glock and thought about his offer. She really didn't want to wait until morning to get out there and prove that she'd seen a body being dumped. She knew what she'd seen.

Narrowing her gaze, she pinned him with a hard look. "Do you have scuba equipment?"

He nodded. "Are you certified to dive? At night?"

Her PADI—Professional Association of Diving Instructors—certification had expired years ago. And she'd never gotten around to getting her night-dive certification. "Are you?" she countered.

"I am."

"Would you be willing to dive down?"

He flashed a grin. "Would be my pleasure."

Now, why did his words give her pause? Why was he so eager to help? "Fine, I'll take you up on the offer. But keep your hands to yourself. And no sudden movements."

"Oh, you can trust me."

"I could, but I don't."

His blue eyes twinkled. "I'd be shocked if you did. Considering you're a cop and all." He strode to the boat and untied the ropes from the dock. "Come on, I won't bite," he coaxed. "I promise."

Hoping she wasn't making a mistake, Angie followed. Glad she'd brought her personal firearm with her, she placed her hand back on her weapon. Just in case Jason decided to renege on his promise.

Aware that his attractive guest was as nervous as a long-tailed cat on a porch full of rocking chairs, Jason started the engine and smoothly maneuvered the *Regina Lee* away from the dock.

Covertly, he glanced over at the detective. He liked the way her brunette hair was pulled back into a wild puff of curls and the way her brown eyes, the color of chicory coffee, observed everything. Her lithe figure moved with grace and agility beneath her denim cropped pants and V-neck T-shirt.

Her peaches-and-cream complexion barely hinting at a touch of sun suggested she hadn't been on the island long. She'd told the chief she was a Boston homicide detective. Her accent attested to that fact. She sounded like she'd been born and raised in Bean Town, too.

She made a credible witness. Yet, she'd been brushed off by the chief like a bothersome mosquito. Curious.

The deck boat the detective had described sounded similar to one reported to be in use by Picard. For the past six months, Jason had relentlessly pursued every lead to find the elusive arms dealer, who, after fleeing

New Mexico, was rumored to have landed here on Loribel Island.

Jason was champing at the bit to find the man and take him down, but Picard was being protected now by the very government that had sought to arrest him. The elusive Picard had become a source of intel into terrorist activity in the States and abroad. Rage simmered low in Jason's belly. He couldn't move until he could identify Picard and find something concrete to nail him with, something the government couldn't ignore. Then Garrett's death would be avenged.

Jason hoped this situation with the pretty cop witnessing something so very odd could turn out to be the catalyst that brought Picard out into the open. Weapons were Picard's specialty. But taking Picard down for murder would do just as well.

Now he just needed Angie to show him where she'd seen the bag dropped.

Slowly, as if to obey the no wake rule, Jason headed the Bayliner Bowrider, a boat designed for day cruising, in the direction the vacationing cop had indicted to Chief Decker. A breeze kicked up, churning the ocean and creating small swells. Indications of the storm to come.

"Angie—can I call you Angie?"

For a moment she pursed her lips before nodding.

Jason found himself fascinated with her full mouth and the little freckle at its corner. He tore his gaze away to focus on the water ahead. "You wouldn't happen to know the coordinates of where you saw the guys in the boat drop the bag, would you?"

"I'm not a sailor."

Amusement had him smiling. Of course she wasn't. She was a pretty, hard-edged cop. "Thought I'd ask."

"Veer more to the left," she said as she came to stand beside him at the helm. "Slow down."

"Where were you when you saw the boat?"

"Sitting on the deck of my aunt's cottage." She pointed toward a row of lights dotting the shoreline.

The shadowy night sky made discerning the outline of any individual house impossible. "It's too dark now to see which one is Aunt Teresa's, but I think we're just about where I saw the boat stop."

He cut the engine, letting the boat bobble with the current while he dug out his dive apparatus. He could only hope he'd find some evidence to link to Picard at the bottom of the ocean.

She moved to the side railing and looked overboard. "I see why the chief wanted to wait until morning," she muttered.

"No worries. I've an underwater light," he said.

The sound of another boat approaching grabbed Jason's attention. A deck boat, illuminated by high-powered lights attached to the sides, sliced through the choppy water.

Jason abandoned the dive equipment to stand beside Angie. "Is that the same boat?"

"I don't think so. The one I saw was bigger with a higher top deck," she said. "Who do you think they are?"

Trepidation slithered over him as the boat closed in.

"Not sure. Help me put this stuff back into the cargo hold," he said, not wanting to advertise their purpose in being out on the water.

Together they made short work of restoring the scuba equipment. "Let me do the talking," Jason said as the boat slowed.

"They're armed," Angie said in a tight voice.

"Yeah," he acknowledged as a hard knot formed in his chest.

Men carrying submachine guns stood at the fore and aft positions. Another man, flanked on either side by two more armed guards, called out instructions to the driver.

Apprehension tethered Jason's feet to the deck. He swallowed back a prayer for help. No need to waste hope that God would come through for him. Jason would just have to make sure he and Angie got through this alive on his own.

The boat drew abreast of the *Regina Lee*.

TWO

Forcing himself to relax, Jason worked his cover persona, deepening his Southern drawl. "Island Charters at your service."

Two armed men wearing jeans and black T-shirts jumped aboard as the wake of the other boat rocked the *Regina Lee*.

"What in the world?" Angie said, reaching for her gun.

Jason caught her hand and held on tight even as she jerked to free herself from his hold. He pulled her slightly behind him to keep her out of the men's line of vision. In a low voice meant for her ears only, he growled, "Stand down."

She stilled. He didn't have to see her glare; he felt it, but he stayed focused on the men with the guns.

"Hey, not cool to board a man's boat without permission," Jason said.

Ignoring him, the men scrutinized the interior of the boat, going so far as to open the cabin door and peer inside. What were they looking for?

The man who seemed to be in charge stepped closer to the railing. Jason didn't recognize the tall, muscular Hispanic man. Could he be Picard?

No. Felix wouldn't be so careless as to show himself. Still, Jason memorized the face. Angular jawline, dark eyes slightly rounded at the edges, wide bridge across the nose, scar over the right eye. Jason would have an ID on the guy in no time once he returned to his rented condo near the marina.

Were these Picard's men? Or was there another illegal entity working out of Loribel?

"What are you doing out here?" the man asked in a thick Spanish accent.

"I'm taking the lady on a night cruise around the island."

"Why'd you stop here?"

"She thought she saw a dolphin." Jason shrugged. "You know tourists. Easily fascinated."

"There're no dolphins. Move along."

"Sure, whatever you say." Ignoring Angie's low growl of disapproval, Jason turned to the two men who'd boarded his boat. "You coming with us?"

The two looked to their boss for direction. With a flick of his hand, the boss indicated for the men to return to the other boat.

Relieved not to have the unwanted guests, Jason practically dragged Angie to the helm with him, careful to keep her back to the men.

Thankfully, she remained silent, but the faint moonlight revealed the fiery expression that said she wanted to confront the situation head-on. Not a good idea when they were outmanned and outgunned.

He started the engine and pushed the throttle forward, easing the boat away from the other craft before letting the throttle out and speeding back toward the marina.

He glanced back only once. The deck boat was now only a bright dot in the dark. He hadn't seen dive equipment on board but that didn't mean there hadn't been any. In any case, he would return to the spot in the morning before Decker and dive down just in case the bag was still there.

Angie brought out her cell phone. "I don't have a signal yet. Not even roaming."

Jason took the phone from her hands, noticing again the strength in her long tapered fingers. "You don't want to call this in. Just let it go. You're on vacation. You should act like it."

"I can't let it go." Her voice held an incredulous note. "I can't let those men get away with intimidation. Not to mention those weapons. They were there to get the body. I have to tell Chief Decker."

Jason shook his head. "I don't think you saw a body being dumped."

"You don't believe me?"

The hurt in her tone unexpectedly twisted inside Jason's chest. "I believe you saw something. Something worth sending out armed men to retrieve. And the less people who know you saw anything the better. Believe me—you don't want to mess with those men."

"If it wasn't a body, then what? Drugs? Weapons?"

"Hard to say," he said in a dismissive tone. The woman wasn't going to relent, was she? "The Colombian drug cartel has a pipeline to the U.S. through the Keys. Arms dealers are a dime a dozen, especially around the Gulf of Mexico."

"But wouldn't the salt water ruin drugs or weapons?"

"Not necessarily, if they were secured in airtight, waterproof packaging."

She peered at him with suspicion in her eyes. "You're not a simple boat captain. Who are you?"

Her hand rested on her hip, where her holstered weapon was concealed beneath her waistband. There was no doubt in his mind she wouldn't hesitate to draw on him if she thought he was a criminal. But for her own good, he couldn't reveal his identity.

"You don't think I'm simple?" He placed a hand over his heart. "That warms me. It really does."

She rolled her eyes and pushed a stray curl out of her face. "Be serious. Who are you?"

"I'm always serious."

Irritation gleamed in the swirling depths of her eyes. "I want an answer."

"Bossy, much?"

She stared him down, hard. A look meant to intimidate. He'd bet she'd used that look on suspects and witnesses. Probably got people talking. He enjoyed baiting her. But he really needed her to take the situation seriously. If she kept pushing, she'd find out how dangerous things could get.

The image of Garrett, dying in his arms, shuddered through his consciousness. He banked the memory and sobered. "Look, I've been at this a long time. These waters are infested with sharks. The human kind. Trust me, you'll be safer if you pretend you didn't see anything."

"No can do." She relaxed her stance slightly. "I've sworn an oath to uphold the law."

He let up on the throttle and slowed to the minimum speed as the boat entered the marina limits. "Honorable. But down here, you don't have jurisdiction. Besides, once Chief Decker searches and finds nothing, you'll have lost credibility."

"Exactly why I am going tell him about the men now," she argued. She held out her hand. "My phone."

Easing the *Regina Lee* into her slip, he cut the engine before handing over her phone. "Your funeral."

She made a face, which he found charming, as she swiped the phone, and then hopped off the boat onto the dock. Jason shook his head with exasperation and admiration. The woman was a spitfire determined to do the right thing. He couldn't blame her. But she had no idea what kind of hornets' nest she'd stumbled into.

Whether Picard or some other lowlife, those men on the boat meant business. A lone lady cop out of her element and her jurisdiction wasn't a match.

That meant it was up to Jason to keep Detective Carlucci safe.

He gritted his teeth to keep from swearing, a habit he'd been trying to break for years. Why did foul words rise so easily when he was frustrated?

Out of the mouths of men came the issues of the heart.

Jason could just hear Garrett's voice piping into his mind. Even from the grave his friend was trying to save him. Anger and frustration were things Jason and God were working on. Some days there were small victories. Other days, not so much.

After quickly tying off the boat, Jason went after the pretty detective. He found her opening the door of her rental convertible.

"Nice ride," he commented. "You know how to vacation in style."

Frowning, she asked, "What do you want now?"

He chose not to take offense at her annoyed tone. "I take it your call to the chief didn't go well?"

Turning away, she closed her eyes for a moment. "He said I could come in and make a report."

Not the response she'd obviously been hoping for. "Are you going to?"

Her lips twisted. "Would it do any good?"

"I don't think so." He hoped she wouldn't push this. For her safety. And for his mission. "You did your duty. You informed the local law enforcement. Nothing else can be done."

"I guess."

She stared out at the dark ocean. "How long has Decker been Chief?"

"A while now." Decker had been elected a few months prior to Jason's arrival. The guy had checked out.

"You think he's competent?"

"I think this is a small island with a low crime rate."

"And I'm just a hassle."

He hated how deflated she sounded. He rather liked her spunk. "Hey, forget about him. How about I buy you a late dinner."

Peering at him with speculation, she said, "No, thanks. Shouldn't I be paying you for taking me out?"

"Naw." He waved a hand.

"Not a very smart business move, don't you think?"

Oh, but she was quick. And he needed to remember to maintain his cover. "I can afford it."

He didn't mention the excursion was on the government's dime.

"Business that good, huh? Even in this economy?"

"What can I say? Tourism may be down elsewhere in the world, but not here on Loribel."

"Right." She slid into the car and turned the key. "I'm sure I'll see you around."

He stepped back so she could pull the convertible out of the parking space. As the red glow of the car's taillights disappeared into the night, he said aloud, "Count on it."

He'd be keeping an eye on the pretty detective for as long as she was on the island.

And he hoped that wasn't going to be very long. He really didn't want the distraction. Forming any sort of attachment wasn't part of Jason's game plan. Work and women didn't mix. Even ones as pretty and spirited as Angie Carlucci.

Angie entered the darkened cottage and paused to listen before turning on the lights. Her internal warning system stayed quiet. No discernible threat waited in the shadows. Still, she kept her hand on the weapon at her waist as she flipped on the light, locked the door and searched the premises, to assure herself all was as she'd left it.

She let out a relieved breath.

Going to the kitchen to fix herself a tuna sandwich, she scoffed at her own silly paranoia. The armed men on the boat had rattled her more than she'd expected or cared to admit. For several heart-throbbing moments she'd been afraid. Only the silent prayers she'd sent heavenward had allowed her to keep her composure.

Fear was not something that could be allowed. Fear could mean death. Hers or others'.

But Jason had hardly seemed unnerved by the boat of armed men.

Except when he was barking orders at her to stand down. He'd sounded exactly like her academy instructors. What was up with that?

Ex-military? That would explain how nonplussed he'd been. And how autocratic.

At first she'd chafed against the obvious he-man tactic he'd employed by pulling her behind him as if she were some damsel in distress. Okay, maybe a bit of distress, but still—

If those men had wanted them dead, Jason's body would hardly have been an effective defense. Though in retrospect, she realized he'd been trying to protect her, not as a fragile flower but rather to shield her identity from the men on the boat.

So they wouldn't come after her because of what she'd seen? She shuddered at the thought.

She hadn't expected gallantry from a total stranger, but there it was. Tenderness welled up. The man might be a bit irritating, but he'd shown a streak of honor she couldn't deny. Definitely military material. And good-looking. Very good-looking. Muscular but not overly. Strong, capable hands. And a slow, killer smile that knocked the wind out of her lungs.

Forcing Jason from her thoughts, she took her food out to the back deck. A gust of wind threatened to rip the plate from her hand. She tightened her grip and stared out at the ocean to the spot where she'd seen the black bag go into the water. She burned with curiosity and the need to prove to Chief Decker and Jason that what she'd seen was worth investigating.

What if those men who'd chased them away hadn't been able to find the bag? It could still be at the bottom of the ocean.

Angie sure could use a boat of her own. And scuba gear. She'd have to wait until morning to rent either one. But would she be early enough to get out on the ocean before Chief Decker? Doubtful.

She sliced a look to her left where there was a storage door underneath the cottage's eaves. Maybe her aunt had something she could use.

Setting her plate on the small round table beside the Adirondack chair, she tried the knob. Locked.

She ran inside for the keys Aunt Teresa had sent her. There were two keys. One fit the front and back doors. The other had to open the storage closet.

Sure enough, the key slid easily into the lock. With the door open, she felt around the inside wall until she found a light switch. Score.

A single-person sit-on-top kayak was fastened to the wall by bungee cords. Several shelves lined the wall filled with beach gear.

The kayak wasn't ideal. She'd only ever kayaked down the Charles River, which was a far cry from the agitated water of the ocean. But she wasn't going to let a little thing like inexperience stop her.

She held a paddle in one hand and snorkel gear in the other and made a decision. As soon as the sun rose she'd paddle out. Obviously, she wouldn't be able to go very deep with a snorkel but she wasn't planning on dredging the bag up. She'd leave that to Decker and his men. All she wanted to do was confirm what she'd seen.

She'd show Mr. Jason Bodewell that a Carlucci never gave up on an investigation.

Beneath a sky streaked with gold and safety-cone orange, Jason eased the *Regina Lee* away from the dock. He searched the horizon for the impending tropical storm predicted on the news. Other than the wind gusting over the Gulf water, he didn't see any signs. But that didn't mean one wasn't brewing. Sometimes they came on fast and left a trail of destruction in their wake. But not yet.

Once clear of the marina, he sped toward the apex of the coordinates he'd memorized last night, while keeping a sharp eye out for any unwanted attention. Especially a boat full of armed men.

He doubted he'd find anything at the bottom of the ocean; the men in the boat wouldn't have left anything of value behind. But one never knew.

And it gave him something to do. He was so tired of waiting. Waiting for Picard to slip up and show his hand. Chatter through the intricate intel channels monitored by both ICE—U.S. Immigration and Customs Enforcement—and ATF—Bureau of Alcohol, Tobacco, Firearms and Explosives—solidified the belief that Picard was on Loribel Island.

Posing as a charter-boat captain allowed Jason to explore the coastline all the way around the island. He had narrowed down three possible places Picard could be working from, since the arms dealer would need ocean access. All were being monitored by satellite surveillance. Which hadn't yielded much so far.

But now that Jason had identified the man from last night as Hector Ramirez, a name linked with Picard in Interpol files, Jason was sure it would only be a matter of time before he found Ramirez again. Jason prayed the man would lead him to Picard.

Up ahead, a small craft, maybe a kayak, bobbed in the waves. Jason slowed the *Regina Lee,* his gaze sweeping the area. About fifty yards from the kayak, a dark head popped up, breaking through the waves. Water spurted out of a snorkel.

Jason stared as disbelief and frustration built in his chest. There was no mistaking the face staring at him from behind a clear mask.

"Women," he muttered, making the word sound like an epithet.

Putting down anchor helped calm his ire. Moving to the side of the boat, he called out, "What are you doing?"

With graceful, broad strokes, Angie swam closer. She had on a short-sleeved black dive suit similar to his own. When she reached the *Regina Lee,* she lifted the mask to rest on her forehead and blinked up at him. "Enjoying the water. You?"

His mouth quirked. "The same."

She smiled, clearly not believing him any more than he believed her. "Did you see anything of note?"

She shook her head. "No." She held up the snorkel. "I was hoping I'd be able to see the bottom but it's too murky."

He reached behind him to where his scuba gear sat on the floor of the boat and held it up for inspection. "I can take care of that."

"I'd appreciate it."

"You might want to grab your kayak before it floats away," he pointed out, watching the drifting craft move farther out to sea.

"Ugh, I had it tied to my wrist," she exclaimed and swam away, powerful and lithe in the water.

Jason couldn't deny he liked the lady cop. She was determined and persistent. Good qualities, but ones that could get her hurt. Not something he was going to let happen.

Slipping the tank onto his back, he donned the dive mask and breathing apparatus, readying himself for the dive.

Glancing around to make sure no boats were approaching, he slipped over the side and into the water. He swam down to the ocean floor, careful to check the depth meter on his watch so as not to go beyond the limit and risk nitrogen poisoning.

At fifty feet he could see the ocean floor. Sediment and sand swirled with the current, seaweed danced in clumps and fish scattered. He searched for several minutes. Nothing. He rose slowly, letting his body adjust to avoid decompression sickness.

At the surface, he found Angie treading water while using one hand to hold the kayak in place.

"Anything?" she asked, her voice eager.

"Nope. Didn't really expect to see anything."

"Right." She stripped off the snorkel gear and tossed it into the seat of the kayak. "Thanks for trying."

Did she think he'd done this for her? Interesting. And useful for hiding his true motivations. "You're welcome. I figured you'd be itching until you knew for sure. I just hadn't expected to find you out here already."

"Tenacious as a bulldog, or so my father likes to tell me," she said with a self-effacing grimace.

"A good quality in a detective," he replied as he kicked his legs to remain upright, the weight of the tank heavy on his back. "Hey, why don't we finish this conversation on my boat."

For a moment indecision warred in her lovely brown eyes. "Don't you have some tourists to motor around the island?"

Oh, man. His cover. *Dude, you're slipping.* "Not today. The weatherman predicts a storm." He hoped she bought the flimsy excuse. "I'm all yours."

She blinked and turned away. "Right, a storm."

He studied her profile, liking the straight line of her nose, the high cheekbones and long-lashed eyes, so natural in the morning light. "So can I give you a lift?"

Slowly, she nodded.

"Great." He moved closer to help her with the kayak.

Together they towed the kayak to the *Regina Lee.* Jason was acutely aware of her beside him. When their legs brushed against each other beneath the surface of the water, a wave of shock jolted his system. Not good. Not good at all.

The last thing he needed was to let attraction derail his mission. He needed to stay focused and professional. Romance and undercover work didn't mix well. A painful lesson he'd already learned.

Purposefully, he distanced himself from her as they worked together to maneuver the kayak onto the back of the boat.

Once Jason was on board, he grabbed towels from a cupboard in the cabin and handed one to Angie.

She took the towel with a grateful smile. "Thanks."

Keeping his gaze from following the towel's progress over her limbs, Jason started the engine but let the boat idle. "So now will you let this situation go?"

She sat on the padded bench near the helm. "I've not much choice now, do I?"

Relieved to hear she had come to that conclusion on her own, he relaxed. "How long are you planning on staying on Loribel?"

She lifted her shoulder in a negligent shrug. "Supposed to be a week, but…"

"But?"

"I don't vacation well."

That made him chuckle. "Yeah, so I've seen." He really liked her. What would it hurt to spend a little time with her before she left? "I'm starved. How about I treat you to breakfast?"

Tilting her head to the side slightly, she regarded him intently. "Why are you being so nice to me?"

"I shouldn't be?"

"What's in it for you?"

"You're never off duty, are you?"

She raised a nicely arched, dark eyebrow in reply.

He conceded the point with a laugh. "Can't a guy ask a pretty lady to breakfast, especially after what we've shared?"

The corners of her mouth tipped up but her eyes

showed doubt. "I suppose. Though I'd be more comfortable if I could put on some dry clothes."

"Ah. Tell you what, we'll moor the boat at the marina and I'll drive you in my Jeep to your place. You can freshen up and then we'll head into Old Town Loribel. I know the best place to get fresh seafood omelets."

She contemplated him a moment before answering.

"Deal." She sat back, letting her head rest against the side of the boat, her eyes drifting closed.

Jason smiled with satisfaction. Today would be a nice, calm day. A day where he could just be a guy enjoying a lady's company. He had to admit the prospect was tantalizing since he couldn't remember the last time he'd allowed himself a day off. That was one of the many things his ex-fiancée had complained about.

After mooring the boat, Jason went into the cabin to change into a pair of khaki cargo shorts, a button-up printed shirt and rugged Teva sandals.

They made the short drive to her place, where he waited in the Jeep while she ran inside the cottage to change. She came out wearing cropped, powder-blue cotton pants with a matching short-sleeved zipped-up jacket. Her dark hair was still pulled back from her face, the ends twisted up and captured by a gold clip. He detected the telltale bulge of her holster at her waist.

Did she ever really relax?

He silently snorted. Like he ever really did. They made quite a pair.

Twenty minutes later, dry and seated at a corner booth in Celeste's Café, Jason watched Angie over the top of his mug of steaming coffee.

He noticed the small cross dangling from a gold chain around her neck. An ache started in his chest. It had been a while since he'd really thought about God. Not since the night Garrett died. Distrust and anger separated them. Jason didn't know how to breach the barrier and frankly, wasn't sure he wanted to try.

Forcing himself to stay in the moment, he asked Angie, "So tell me how you got into law enforcement."

Toying with the rim of her glass of orange juice, she said, "Family business. Grandfather, father, brothers."

Impressive. "All Boston P.D.?"

"Grandfather and father both retired from the force." She smiled, her eyes crinkling at the corners. "Eldest brother is Secret Service, and the other ATF."

Ah, he'd thought the name *Carlucci* sounded familiar. Special Agent Joseph Carlucci had been part of the joint task force that had tracked Picard in New Mexico. Jason was sure Joseph was still working the southwest corridor. He'd liked the guy. And now felt doubly responsible to make sure Angie left the island in one piece. Preferably sooner rather than later.

"Here comes trouble," Angie said, ducking her head slightly as she stared over his shoulder to the front of the restaurant.

Trepidation curled low in his belly. "What?"

"Don't turn around, but one of the armed men from last night just walked in."

Jason grimaced. So much for time off.

THREE

In a swift movement that startled Angie, Jason's hand closed over her wrist, the pressure pinning her hand to the table. "Don't even think about it."

His hard, knowing expression bathed in a shaft of morning light streaming through the café's window stilled her breath. How could he read her so well? She didn't even try to play innocent. "I'm not going to just let the guy walk around free. We need to detain him and call Chief Decker."

Jason's sooty blue-gray eyes narrowed. "You really want to start something in here? The guy's probably not alone."

Snapping to attention, she scanned the restaurant, searching for a threat. The other patrons seemed innocuous enough. A family of four sat at a middle table, the children both still half-asleep.

An older couple sat by the window. The man read the paper while the wife stared out at the beach. At the counter, two men and a woman ate breakfast while joking with the waitress.

Angie didn't see anyone who looked to be in cahoots with the gunman. "I can handle him and anyone else," she replied.

"And risk other people's lives?"

Jason's question brought her gaze back to him and the censure in his expression. Indignation rose to settle in her chest. How could he even suggest she'd put innocent lives in jeopardy? She'd sworn an oath to protect and serve. She took her vow seriously.

Frowning, she settled back against the booth's cushioned seat, while keeping an alert eye on the male subject in question as he walked toward a table on the other side of the room. Thankfully, he'd sat with his back to them. There was a chance the man could ID her and Jason. They'd have to be careful.

Mentally she cataloged the suspicious man's description—five foot ten, two hundred pounds, dark hair, jeans, work boots and plain green T-shirt. Just below the hem of the right sleeve, the edges of a tattoo winked at her. The guy didn't appear to be carrying, but that didn't mean he wasn't.

Feeling Jason's stare pressing on her, she said, "Then what do you suggest?"

He glanced over his shoulder. "He doesn't seem to be going anywhere at the moment." Turning back around, he said, "We watch him. See where he goes. Maybe he'll lead us to the others."

Was that a note of veiled excitement in his voice? "What are you, a thrill junkie?"

A brief, amused smile flashed before he said, "I

believe in making the most of opportunities presented."

Sounded like something her brothers would say. But they were in the business of seeking opportunities to take down bad guys. What was Jason's motivation? She needed more background info on the amiable boat captain. A lot more. Looked like she'd be calling Gabe, her Boston P.D. partner, to do a background check.

She hoped Jason didn't have a record or a warrant anywhere. She was beginning to really like the guy.

And maybe he was right. Maybe they should be patient and sit tight. But she never did watch and wait well. Patience wasn't one of her virtues. Probably one of the many character flaws that had sent men running in the other direction. That and her career. Would Jason run from her? Did she care?

"Tell me about yourself," she said.

"Not much to tell," he responded and studied the menu.

She arched a brow. They'd already ordered their meal.

"Come on. Talk to me." She reached across the table to put her hand over the menu to gain his attention. "Who is Jason Bodewell? Are you ex-military?"

Setting the menu to the side, he gave her his attention. "Yeah, I've served my country."

"Which branch?"

"Army."

From the guarded tone of his voice, she guessed his service had left scars. "Did you grow up here on the island?"

"No. Born and bred in a small town outside Jackson, Mississippi."

Now she understood why his accent was so much thicker than any she'd heard so far while on vacation. "You're a long way from home."

His expression dimmed as sadness deepened the blue of his eyes. "Nothing there for me anymore. My parents passed on. I don't have siblings."

Her stomach clenched with remembered panic and dread of her father's heart attack last year. Sympathy for Jason infused her. She wanted to reach out and hold him, to soothe away his pain. "I'm sorry. How old were you when they died?"

"My dad passed on when I was a kid. Emphysema. He was a chain smoker for as long as I can remember. My mom—" His voice hitched. "She died of breast cancer about eight years ago."

Compassion twisted in her chest. She couldn't imagine having both parents die so young. "You don't have any other family?"

He paused, his expression turning distant. Hard. "Not anymore."

Their food arrived, preventing further questioning but not alleviating the curiosity churning in her mind. What was Jason's story? Was his military background his only reason for getting involved with her and this situation?

As she contemplated the questions, she ate her pancakes quickly. Sweet maple syrup exploded on her taste buds with each bite. She wanted to be ready to move the moment the gunman from last night decided to leave the café.

"Guess you were hungry," Jason commented. His amused gaze flicked to her empty plate.

She shrugged. "Need to be ready."

"Ah, I see," he said.

Taking her cue, his seafood omelet disappeared rapidly. She appreciated how in tune he was with the situation. But really she shouldn't expect him to put his job and life at risk to help her. Even though he was ex-army, he was now a civilian. Or was he? The question lingered in her mind, trying to take shape. But nothing beyond his mannerism suggested he was on active status. She shrugged the notion off.

"Let's go. We can position ourselves outside," he said as he laid down cash to pay the bill.

Careful to keep her face turned away from the gunman, Angie followed Jason out of the café. The morning's air had grown thick, making her cotton jacket stick to her skin. Ominous clouds darkened the sky. A gust of wind ruffled the trees and bushes along the landscaped main street of Old Loribel. Jason led her to a park bench beneath the cover of a red maple tree. Though the branches offered some protection from the storm, it did nothing to relieve the humidity that she was becoming used to.

She sat on the edge of the bench. Awareness of his presence pulsed through her. He had a ruggedness and a vital power that drew her in, making her wish he'd sit beside her and wrap his arm around her shoulders for an embrace. Her face flushed hot with embarrassment. "You don't have to stay. I can handle this alone. I'm sure you have somewhere to be."

"There isn't anyplace on earth I'd rather be." His intense gaze hinted at some deeper meaning, despite the playful curve of his mouth.

Taken aback by his words, her heart fluttered uncharacteristically beneath her breastbone. The man was charming to be sure, but there was something else, something in his steel gaze that made her believe his words. Trills of excitement raced up her spine, but self-doubt trampled after, warning, "Don't get your hopes up."

Needing to bring the conversation to a more benign topic, she asked, "What brought you to Loribel Island?"

Jason stretched his long legs out in front of him as he settled next to her and rested an arm along the back of the bench. "Many things. The ocean, the sun. It's usually a peaceful place." He slanted a mischievous glance at her. "But then you arrived."

"Wow," she said with a playful tone. "Thanks."

Attraction arced. She forced her gaze from his teasing grin and focused on the café. He was gorgeous. Fine. But just because she was acutely responsive to him didn't mean she had to be interested. Did it? And if she was—where could a romance possibly lead? Her life was in Boston, his here on Loribel.

The door to the café had opened, and the man they were waiting for walked out.

Jason stiffened, his whole body seeming to vibrate with energy. "Here we go."

Senses jumping to alert, she smothered her romantic musings and concentrated on their quarry. They followed him, careful to keep a reasonable distance.

The man led them through Old Loribel, past quaint boutiques and art galleries that might tempt distraction for others, but to her were potential places where the suspicious man or his accomplices could hide.

Pausing occasionally beside the tall, graceful palms lining the street, Angie found Jason an easy surveillance partner. It had taken her and her currant homicide detective partner, Gabe Burke, at least a month before they'd synced.

Not once did she have to pull Jason back or explain the subtlety of feigning interest in anything other than the subject. Obviously he hadn't forgotten his army training. Still, she had to wonder why he was going along with her. What was in it for him?

When they reached the parking lot at the end of town and the man climbed into a beat-up, red, single-cab truck, Angie figured they'd lose the guy. Jason's Jeep was back near the café. But Jason surprised her by procuring two touring bikes from a nearby rental stand.

"Seriously?" She stared at the bright pink helmet he handed her.

"What better way to blend in than to stick out." He grinned and secured a neon green helmet on his head.

Knowing precious seconds were ticking by, Angie didn't argue. She quickly let down her hair to don the helmet and hopped on the bike. Keeping the truck in sight, she started down the road, her legs pumping the pedals and her heart rate kicking up with the effort. The invigorating sense of action and adrenaline propelling Angie forward made her smile. Jason rode beside her, falling back when traffic demanded.

The clouds let loose with a smattering of rain. Her excitement wasn't dampened even as wetness soaked her clothes.

A bike chase was definitely a first—one her brothers would get a kick out of.

She glanced at Jason. He winked. Exhilaration bubbled over into a laugh.

Two miles later, the red truck turned off the main street onto a paved private road, then disappeared from view behind thick, lush foliage lining the road.

Frustrated, Angie pulled over to the muddy shoulder and stopped. A second later Jason halted beside her.

"Do you know where that road leads?" she asked.

His expression grew pensive. "Oh, yeah. There's an estate at the end that belongs to the Corrinda family. They've been here since the founding of the island." His gaze narrowed in speculation. "There's a private cove attached to the property."

Anticipation revved in her veins. "Let's go."

"No." He grabbed the handlebar of her bike. "It's private property."

She opened her mouth to say the restrictions didn't matter, she had probable cause. Those men last night had illegal weapons. Only, she didn't have jurisdiction. Here she'd be nothing more than a trespasser. She yanked her cell phone out of her jacket pocket. "I'll call the chief."

"Definitely one option. But really, what's the chief going to do? You didn't file a report. He's not going to raid a private residence without probable cause. And the way he dismissed you before, I doubt he'd take your word alone."

Her gut twisted with frustration and unease. He was right. Chief Decker hadn't exactly been very receptive last night. But with Jason's collaboration the chief would have to take her seriously. "You can back me up."

He shook his head, his stormy eyes troubled. "Sorry. No way do I want to get involved with the authorities."

Disbelief and anger rushed to batter at her temples just as the rain beat against the helmet and soaked her clothes. "Why?"

"Hey, I'm just a boat captain trying to make a living while having a little fun in the sun."

So that's what all of his help was about—him having some fun. At her expense.

Disappointment clawed at her insides. He wasn't the man she thought he was. "Fine. You don't need to be involved. I'll go see Chief Decker by myself."

She yanked the bike from his grasp and pedaled back toward town, not bothering to see if Jason followed.

Jason's insides coiled with guilt as he watched Angie ride away. For the first time in his life he regretted having to play the part his undercover work demanded. Boy, was he having a hard time keeping up the pretense with Angie.

He'd been apologetic to Serena when he'd had to leave and couldn't tell her anything about the assignment.

But why did he regret keeping his cover with a woman he'd just met and barely knew?

He could only guess it was because she was a fellow law-enforcement officer. If he could take her into his confidence, he would in a heartbeat. But he'd worked too hard and too long to build this cover. Even one person knowing his true identity could jeopardize the whole mission. No way would he risk blowing everything because he liked the pretty cop.

The faster she left the island the better. She was proving to be a distraction he really couldn't afford. He could never forget his purpose. And with Angie around he might.

He rode back to town, letting Angie stay well ahead of him but maintaining a visual on her. He still had an obligation to protect her. At the bike rental hut, he stopped her from walking away. "Let me drive you back to your place."

She shook off his hand. "That's okay. I'll manage. Just steer me in the direction of the police department."

There was no point in refusing her request. He gestured to the brick building off the main street with the American flag flying out front. "There."

She walked away without another word.

Jason might not want to tip his hand to the local LEOs—law-enforcement officers—but he wasn't going to just let Angie run around the island unprotected. He waited beneath the cover of an ancient Banyan tree, its curving branches and wide leaves giving some relief from the rain.

Taking his iPhone from his shirt pocket, he typed out a message to his SAC—Special Agent in Charge of the ICE Office of Investigations field office in D.C.—telling him about the lead and asking for more info on the Corrinda family. Were they connected to Picard? Or had they started some kind of illegal operation of their own?

When Angie came out of the station ten minutes later, he could tell by the angry set of her shoulders and the red in her cheeks that her talk with the chief hadn't been productive. A good thing for him but he felt bad for her. He fell into step with her.

"What are you still doing here?" she snapped as she stalked down the road.

He liked the way her nose wrinkled up when she was irritated. "I've nothing else to do today because of the storm."

"Lucky me."

"I take it the chief is still being difficult?"

She slanted him a withering glare. "The man is insufferable and chauvinistic. He had the gall to suggest I was making everything up"

Jason grimaced at the hurt underlining her words. He wasn't sure why the chief would be so dismissive. He could only guess Decker didn't want Detective Carlucci intruding on his territory. Which was good for Jason. Not so good for Angie's ego.

She stopped and glanced around as if suddenly realizing she didn't know where she was going. The disconcerted expression on her lovely face made Jason yearn to take her in his arms and soothe away her troubles. Instead, he stuffed his hands into his pockets to keep from reaching out to her.

Her mocha-colored eyes met his. "Can you give me that ride back to the cottage?"

"Of course," he said and steered her toward his parked Jeep.

He opened the passenger door for her. She hesitated, glancing down at her soaking clothes.

"Don't worry about getting the seat wet. It happens all the time."

"Thanks," she replied and slid in.

Once they were headed out of town, Jason decided the storm might just be the catalyst to chase Angie off the island. "Too bad about the storm. Maybe now would be a good time to head home before this baby turns into a full-blown hurricane."

She frowned. "Are you trying to get rid of me, too?"

"Not a lot to do during a storm," he said, not liking how dejected she sounded or that he wanted to make her feel better.

Pointing to the ocean, she said, "They don't seem to be bothered by the storm."

He glanced at the day cruisers and fishing boats dotting the water's surface. "Idiots."

As they passed the marina, she turned to him. "Can I hire you for the day?"

He hesitated. Apprehension ruffled his nerves. "What do you have in mind?"

"You said the road we followed the red truck to led to a private cove, right?"

His gut clenched. The eager, determined expression in her lovely brown eyes didn't bode well. He had to respect her tenacity even if he disapproved. "You really need to just let this *go*."

He snapped his fingers. "I know. How about I take you treasure hunting? If you don't mind trudging around in the mud and rain. This island is full of places where old pirates buried their loot, or so the Chamber of Commerce keeps saying."

"I'd rather take a boat tour of the island, including that cove. But if you're not available, I'll find someone else," she said pleasantly.

No way. Anxiety twisted in his chest. He couldn't allow her to involve anyone else. And by the challenge in her expression, she knew he'd surrender. But not for the reason she believed. This wasn't about his ego, this was about the mission and her safety.

If she was determined to take a boat ride, then he'd accommodate her. Taking a recon of the cove wasn't a bad idea and at least he'd have Angie with him so he could keep her out of danger. Though he had a feeling he was the one in trouble. "After the storm passes."

"How long will that be?"

"Could be hours. Could be days." Maybe she'd leave by then. One could hope.

"I'll wait."

He was afraid she'd say that.

The next morning, Jason showed up on Angie's doorstep before sunrise with the news that a break in the storm, which was predicted to last a few hours, made decent enough conditions for a boat tour around the island.

Sitting on the bench along the back of Jason's boat, Angie tried to keep her gaze trained on the shoreline of the other side of the island, but found herself watching Jason instead.

He stood at the wheel, his long legs braced apart, his hand masterfully steering the vessel. Today he wore navy cargo pants and a red windbreaker with the logo of his company emblazoned on the front. She appreciated the look of him but she admired the way he carried himself more, emitting self-confidence and strength. She liked his easygoing manner, yet he'd been protective. Who said chivalry was dead?

There was nothing about Jason that suggested he'd be a man easily intimidated by her career. On the surface, Jason was a man she could see herself falling for. But—she still didn't understand what motivated him or why he was so determined to be her crime-fighting cohort.

Especially after refusing to talk with Chief Decker. There had to be a reason. But what?

Worry churned in her stomach. Was she making a mistake by trusting Jason?

When she'd talked with Gabe, her detective partner, last night, he'd found nothing unseemly in Jason's background. Jason owned the charter company, which comprised the one boat and himself, owned a condo and had a decent enough financial portfolio but nothing to suggest he was involved in anything criminal.

Still something nagged that all was not as it seemed and until she was sure of him, she would keep her heart out of the equation.

"The cove should be up ahead on your left," Jason said, his gaze meeting hers with a direct look that let her know he was aware she'd been staring.

Heat crept into her cheeks. She wasn't sure what he'd seen on her face; she hoped her thoughts of his attractiveness and her misgivings hadn't been transparent. She turned away and shifted on the bench to a better position.

A long stretch of beach with a dock and what looked like a picnic area curved along the coastline until the sand gave way to a more rocky terrain that jutted out to a point, cutting off access to what lay beyond. Above the shore, houses grew out of the lush green foliage covering the hillside. Angie could only imagine the view afforded those blessed with the chance to live on this side of the island. Her aunt's cottage sat closer to the southern tip near the Loribel Lighthouse.

"There." Jason pointed to the wide cove as they moved beyond the rocky point. He slowed then stopped the boat. He came to stand beside Angie.

"Can we get closer?" she asked, squinting but still unable to determine what she was seeing.

"No, but these might help." Jason handed her a pair of black binoculars while keeping a pair for himself.

She flashed him a grateful smile before bringing the ocular lens to her eyes. Adjusting the focus wheel and the diopter brought the cove into clear view.

"Do you recognize either boat?" Jason asked.

She studied the vessels moored in tandem to a long wooden dock. "The farthest one looks like our friends from the night before, don't you think?"

"I do," he said, his tone excited.

"The other boat could be the one I saw dump the bag in the ocean. It looks about the same size and shape. Can you make out the name on the side?"

"*Courir le Soleil.* French for *Race the Sun,*" he translated.

She repeated the words softly to herself. She swung the lens slightly to the right. A large gaping hole in the side of the cove wall came into view. Men moved in and out of the opening like ants. "Hey, what do you think that tunnel is for?"

Following her line of vision, he said, "Interesting. What could they be digging up?"

"Pirate loot?" she quipped, remembering Jason's comment about pirate gold hidden somewhere on the island.

"Maybe. Or they could be burying something." Jason tensed. "We have activity."

Moving the lens of the binoculars slightly up and to the left, she saw a group of armed men exiting from a 20x20 cedar shingled shed that looked as if it were built right into the cliff's wall. As she searched the faces of the men, Angie's breath caught. "I see the guy who was at the café," she exclaimed.

"Yeah, I see him. Uh-oh. We're not the only eyes with binoculars. We've been spotted." Jason dropped the binoculars and moved to the helm, restarted the engine and pushed the throttle forward, sending the boat into motion with a sudden burst.

With mounting apprehension, Angie held on and watched as the tattooed man and several others ran for the boats. "Hurry," she shouted. "They're coming after us."

"Hang on!"

Jason pushed the Bowrider to its limit. The boat shuttered and shook with the speed. He should have gotten them out of there the second he confirmed that deck boat was the same one that had waylaid them the other night. Now they were about to be chased not by one, but two boats full of armed men.

Way to go, Buchett. Jeopardize the whole operation.

His blood ran cold. *And while you're at it put the pretty detective at risk.*

FOUR

Thunder vibrated through the air like the sound of an old steam engine locomotive roaring across the countryside. A sound from Jason's childhood. Good memories, sad memories.

The break in the storm hadn't lasted as long as the weatherman predicted. He glanced at the thickening, dark clouds and pushed the boat to go faster. The last thing he needed was to be struck by lightning. He raced the boat along the ocean's turbulent waters, slicing through the waves and hugging the coast until reaching the busy marina area where the *Regina Lee* could blend in with other Bowriders. He slowed to the no-wake speed and looked for an empty slip.

"I think we lost them," Angie said, her gaze searching the ocean.

"Good." Relief swept over him, easing the tenseness of his shoulders. Still, he wanted to get them out of there. He killed the engine, flipped the buoys over the side and then jumped onto the dock where he quickly tied off the ropes, securing the *Regina Lee* to the dock.

He offered Angie his hand as she climbed from the boat. Her strong fingers grasped his, the pressure sure and confident. He liked the way their palms meshed. They fit together. He held on a little longer than necessary.

Maybe in another place, another life— But wishing for the impossible wasn't productive.

Angie jerked her hand back as soon as her feet were on firm ground, her cheeks blushed becomingly. "I need to call the FBI since the chief won't believe me."

Jason hesitated. Without having to explain his undercover mission, how could he tell her involving the federal authorities wasn't a good idea? He couldn't risk having his identity compromised even to explain the situation to Angie or the Feds. Too many people had worked too long and too hard to build a plausible character that wouldn't draw suspicion.

Only someone truly "deep under" would ever stand a chance of closing in on Picard. He could only fall back on his pretense of not wanting trouble with the authorities and hope she bought his story. "I'm inclined to do as I'm told when men with guns tell me to mind my own business. I would think that would include talking to the law. Besides, you still don't have any proof."

"Right."

The disappointment and censure in her expression cut deep. He didn't like that it seemed as if he was letting her down. She didn't understand what was at stake, and he couldn't fill her in.

He thought of the way her hand fit with his, how perfect and right touching her felt. He gave an inward groan. Her presence was distracting him. Big-time. He needed her gone so he could go back and find out exactly what was going down at that cove without having to worry about her safety.

"Look, it is what it is," he said. "I'm not helping you anymore. Besides, I'm more concerned that those men may be able to identify you and will come after you. You really need to back off." He glanced up at the sky. Storm clouds rolling across the horizon promised a downpour. "In fact, I would recommend leaving the island now before this storm hits full force. The causeway will be a mess before long. The quicker we get you back to your place, the quicker you can pack up and go."

"The storm isn't why you want me to leave." Her eyes narrowed. "You just want to get rid of me so you don't have to babysit me. I can take care of myself. I'm not some prissy Southern belle who appreciates your he-man antics."

She was way too perceptive and a bit off base, but he couldn't let her know. He certainly didn't think of her as prissy or incapable of taking care of herself given the right circumstances, but she was no match for the type of villains bound to come after her if she kept poking her nose where it didn't belong.

And keeping tabs on her would only hinder his progress.

He made a sweeping gesture, encouraging her to notice that all around them boats were being secured as their owners prepared for more wind and rain. "Everyone's going to be running for cover in the next few hours."

"Meanwhile, those men get to roam free." She shook her head. "I can't allow that. It's my job to keep the public safe from the likes of those men with their boatload of illegal guns."

He took a step closer, crowding her. If he had to get mean to keep her safe, so be it. "It may be your job in Boston, but not here. There's no dead body, no witnesses to interview, no suspects to interrogate. The last thing any of us needs is you running around this island chasing danger like a dog chasing a cat. Eventually you'll catch a mouthful. And then what? You're alone. You don't have the law on your side. Those guys wouldn't think twice about killing you, pretty lady or not."

"I'll find my own way back to the cottage."

By way of the cove, no doubt. He reached out to snag her elbow. "I'll drive you."

She yanked her arm away. "No. You've made it clear you're done. I don't need you."

Her angry words ripped through him like shrapnel, stinging in their intensity. Surprise made him flinch. Why did he care? He didn't. The last thing he wanted was for her to need him. "Are you going to leave the island?" he asked, his voice gruff.

"It's really none of your business," she said and turned on her heels to walk away.

She was wrong. It was his business. Because as long as she stayed, he'd feel responsible for her.

He blew out a harsh breath and watched her hurry along the dock toward the marina building, her dark, curly ponytail whipping in the gathering wind. He should follow her to make sure she arrived back at her aunt's cottage safely, though he doubted she would appreciate the effort.

There he went again, being distracted by the lovely Angie. She wasn't his responsibility. He had a job to do. Wasting time arguing with a beautiful, stubborn detective out of her jurisdiction wouldn't accomplish anything productive.

He could only hope she'd make the right choice and scratch investigating the cove off her to-do list before something bad happened to her.

Angie yanked open the door to the marina's main building and stepped inside, her skin instantly cooled by the air conditioner. She glanced around, taking stock. A boat rental sign hung over a long counter and shelves full of groceries and boating paraphernalia crowded the space. A few customers browsed the aisles.

Grateful for the shelter from the angry storm brewing outside, she took a steadying breath. If only the angry storm brewing inside her could so easily be avoided. She didn't get Captain Wishy-washy. Jason's constant change of attitude baffled her. One moment he was gung ho to participate, and the next he was backing off.

If Gabe hadn't already told her the man was what he appeared to be, she'd think Jason had something to hide. She trusted Gabe, but she also trusted her own instincts. And her instincts were screaming that Jason wasn't what he appeared to be.

But what that was, she didn't know. And Angie wasn't sure the effort to find out was worth it when she had something more pressing, like illegal weapons, to investigate.

Forcing Jason from her thoughts, Angie headed toward the counter where an older man with a ruddy complexion stood talking on the phone. Graying hair poked out from beneath the edges of a baseball cap. He wore a long-sleeved T-shirt with a screen print of a basketball player doing a lay-up. He caught Angie's gaze and held up a hand to indicate for her to wait a second.

When he hung up, he smiled, showing stained teeth with badly receding gums. "Hi, there. What can I do for you?"

Angie stuck out her hand. "I'm Angie. I was hoping you could give me some information."

He shook her hand. "Mike. If I can help, I will."

"I want to inquire about a boat," Angie said.

"We're not renting any boats today because of the storm. But they say this squall will pass pretty quickly, so come back in a couple of days," he said.

"I didn't mean I want a boat. I was hoping you could tell me who owns a certain boat." She described the boat. "It has a French name. *Courir le Soleil*," she said, hoping she didn't slaughter the pronunciation too badly.

His expression closed, became guarded. He shook his head. "Sorry. Don't know it."

"What about the Corrinda family? Do you know them?"

"Of course, everyone on the island knows the Corrindas." His gaze narrowed. "Are you a reporter or something?"

"No." Interesting. "Is there something newsworthy going on?"

He shrugged. "Not that I know of. The Corrindas are private people. But every once in a while someone comes on the island wanting to do a piece on them."

"I've heard they've been here for a long time."

"That they have. Old man Corrinda's great-great-grandfather founded the town of Loribel. They own most of the property on the island. Even this here marina belongs to the Corrindas."

"That's a lot of wealth," she mused, wondering just how that wealth was acquired. Buried treasure beneath their estate? She mentally scoffed. Not likely.

"It sure is." The telephone rang. "Excuse me," he said as he moved away to answer. He turned slightly so she couldn't hear the conversation.

The door opened. Wind howled like an angry wolf, reminding Angie of the danger rapidly approaching. She needed to find a ride to her aunt's cottage. Hopefully, Mike would be able to help her out once he was through.

Mike's gaze lifted to someone beyond Angie. She turned to see who'd come inside. Jason walked toward her, carrying a black rain slicker.

She frowned, hating the pleased surprise curling inside her. "I thought you left," she said.

"Not yet. On my way out now."

Mike covered the phone with his palm and called out, "Hey, Jason. Be with you in a sec."

"Hey, Mike," Jason replied and then pointed at Angie. "I'm here for her."

Mike nodded with a wink and then resumed his conversation.

Angie arched an eyebrow at Jason. "Really?"

He gave her one of those devastating grins that knocked the breath right out of her.

"Can I give you a ride?"

Mentally slamming down her reaction, she contemplated his question. She was still mad at him but she did need transportation and he was offering. Now wasn't the time to hold a grudge. "Yes. I'd appreciate it."

"Here." He shoved the slicker toward her. "The rain is coming down hard."

Donning the slicker, she followed him out into the rain, her clothes not protected by the slicker instantly clinging to her skin. His Jeep sat idling, illegally parked at the end of the walkway. They jumped in. The short drive to the cottage took longer than normal because of the storm.

"People really are leaving the island."

"Yes. Did you think I was making that up?"

One corner of her mouth rose. "A little."

"We haven't had an official evacuation warning." He gave her a sidelong glance rife with meaning. "Yet. There's still time for you to go home."

He wanted her gone awfully bad. And it wasn't just the storm driving him. Why? "Mike said he thought this storm would pass quickly."

"Could be. But I'd still advise you to leave now while the weather's relatively calm."

This was relatively calm? Palm trees bent and wobbled in the wind. Gusts rippped around the vehicle so hard Angie could feel the vibrations. Rain pelted the car, pinging loudly on the Jeep's metal exterior.

Jason pulled to a stop in front of the cottage and got out. He walked around to the passenger side as Angie opened the door. The wind whipped the door out of her hand, sending it bouncing on the hinge. For a second she thought it might go flying away.

Jason reached for her hand. "Come on."

Wind swirled over Angie, rattling the slicker as she let him lead her to the front door of the cottage. As she fumbled with the key, Jason disappeared around the back. Curious about what he was doing, she went in search of him. She found him on the back patio, stacking the two Adirondack chairs near the sliding door.

He tugged on the storage-closet door. "Do you have a key for this?"

She nodded and handed over the key ring. He

quickly stored the chairs then unlocked the slider and motioned her inside. She turned on a table lamp near the pullout couch. Wind whistled down the chimney.

"I better go secure my condo," Jason said. "Do you know where a flashlight and candles are in case of a power outage?"

Good question. She headed for the kitchen. "I would imagine there would be some in the drawers."

Jason followed her and helped her search. They found two flashlights in the pantry and a scented candle in the bathroom cupboard, which she placed on the coffee table along with a book of matches from Fiona's Italian Restaurant.

"All set," she announced.

"You're sure you won't reconsider leaving?" Jason stood with his back to the sliding door. Behind him the ocean churned, white-capped waves whipped up by the increasing wind. He looked ruggedly handsome standing there, legs braced apart, his broad shoulders filling the door frame. He looked like he belonged out there braving the elements rather than in her aunt's living room with its provincial furnishings.

"No." Why did he keeping pushing her?

Resignation shone in his blue-gray eyes. "Then I'm sure I'll be seeing you around." He reached for the slider's handle. "If you need anything…" He paused then reached inside the pocket of his windbreaker and pulled out a business card. He set it on the round end table closest to him. "Call."

"Thanks."

He saluted then slipped out the door, leaving Angie more confused. Again he'd offered help, yet he'd been unwilling to do something that could really make a difference. Whatever. She wanted to stop thinking about him, but the image of him standing with the ocean at his back refused to be dismissed.

Stop it, she admonished herself. *Do something useful.*

She decided to call her ATF agent brother, Joe. He'd have access to information on the Corrinda family. Maybe the Feds would be more interested and less likely to have received favors from the Corrinda family than Chief Decker.

She carried a notepad and pen to the dining table and sat in one of the cane-back chairs. Using her cell, she called her brother's work phone. Gotta love roaming. She could feel her bank account draining with each ring.

"Carlucci."

"Hey, Joey, it's Angie."

"Hi there, baby sis. What's up? Mom said you were on vacation in Florida at Aunt Teresa's. Man, I need to do that. Is the cottage the same as when we were kids? Do you remember that one summer when we saw the alligator on the beach? I thought for sure we were goners."

Angie waited a heartbeat to see if her big brother was finished talking before she answered. "Yes, I'm at Aunt Teresa's and yes, the cottage is the same. And I do remember the alligator. I called because I need a favor."

"Anything for you, sis. What do you need?"

"Information on a local family."

"You're supposed to be on vacation, Angie! What kind of information? What family? Is something going on? Do you need me to come down there?"

Years of honed patience made her smile at her brother's barrage of questions. Part of which was his style of communicating but also part of his way of treating her. When they were kids, she'd followed her brothers around like a puppy, desperately wanting to be included in their exciting world of tree forts and sports.

One summer when she was ten, she'd climbed up a huge American elm in hot pursuit of her brothers but had slipped and fallen, breaking her leg and her wrist. From then on, her brothers had tried to coddle and protect her when they didn't need to. Her cross to bear.

And obviously Jason was cut out of the same cloth.

"I'm not in any real trouble," she said, hedging a bit. "No, you don't have to come down here. I just need some background history and anything else you can find on the Corrinda family."

"Why?"

She waited a second, expecting more questions to follow the terse one-word inquiry. When he didn't continue she relayed the events of the past two days, though she left out the part about Jason and his wishy-washy attitude. "It would help if I knew more about them so I can convince the chief to act. It seems like this family has a tight hold on the community."

"Hmm. Sounds like you may have stumbled onto something. I'll see what I can find out and call right back. Stay put, okay?" A note of concern laced his words.

She glanced outside at the wind and rain. "I'm not going anywhere right now." Frustration sizzled through her.

"Good. I'll call soon." He hung up.

Tapping her fingers on the dining table, she made a list, chronicling the events so she'd have a concise record and timeline. Done with that, she looked around for something to occupy her mind.

She went in search of the crossword puzzle book she'd bought the first day she arrived. There was nothing she hated more than to be bored. Crossword puzzles kept her mind active and off the fact she was in fact sitting around waiting.

An hour later, with two crosswords completed, the phone rang. She snatched it before the second ring.

"Hello?"

"It's me," Joey said. "I did some research. This family is mega rich. Not only do they own most of Loribel Island but also several lucrative properties throughout Florida. And they have some holdings in Mexico, Colombia and France, as well."

She jotted down the new information. "Okay. What else?"

"The patriarch and his wife are living on Loribel. They had one son, now deceased. There are two grandsons, Edmund and Erik, who manage the family's money. And there's a granddaughter living in France attending art school. The kid's mother lives in New York."

"Are they under investigation for anything?"

There was a brief pause. "Sis, *if* they were, you know I wouldn't be at liberty to discuss it."

"So ATF *is* interested in this family?"

"I didn't say that. Angie, listen closely. This family has a lot of powerful friends in powerful places. I've made note of what you saw and passed it on. That's all you or I can do. Stay away from the Corrindas and start enjoying your vacation. Or go home."

Taken aback by the harsh tone in her brother's normally congenial voice, Angie said, "You sound like Jason."

"Who? Should I be checking him out, too?"

She rolled her eyes at the barrage of questions. "I had Gabe run a background check. Came up clean." She tugged on her bottom lip with her teeth for a second. "But…there's something about the guy."

"Smitten, are we?"

"What? No," she denied, though her face went hot.

"Hey, I'm not judging. I think it would be great if you found someone special."

"My relationship with him isn't like that."

"Hmm. So there is a relationship. Give me details."

Making a face at her brother's assessment, she said, "His names Jason Bodewell. He runs a charter-boat business. Owns a boat named the *Regina Lee*." She hesitated a second, then plunged in. "Could you see if the federal agencies have anything on him that Gabe couldn't find? Call if there's something I should know about. Otherwise, don't. And thanks for the info on the Corrindas. It's helpful."

"Angie," Joe said with a warning note in his voice. "Promise me you're not going to do anything rash. Let the local LEOs handle this."

"Rash? Me?" She rolled her eyes. "Don't worry, Joey. I've every intention of letting Chief Decker do his thing."

He gave a short laugh. "You better. And be careful."

"Always. Love you. Bye." She hung up.

There was definitely something up with the Corrinda family. If only it was as simple as making the police chief see that.

The four walls of the cottage closed in on her. She hated inactivity, especially when there was a crime to solve. She paced in front of the cold fireplace. Maybe she should go home, go back to her job where she was wanted and appreciated and could be effective.

She should just forget what she'd seen and leave the Corrinda family to others as Joey suggested. Like Chief Decker? Right. The man didn't seem interested at all.

Didn't anyone but her care that the Corrindas employed a small army of armed men who shouldn't be allowed in the civilian realm?

And the bag she'd seen dumped. Had someone else not heeded their warning?

She couldn't let her concerns go.

If she could at minimum capture some photos of the armed men and pass them along to her brother, then she'd at least feel that she'd accomplished something.

Knowing she was probably embarking on a fool's errand because who in their right mind would be out in such bad weather, except perhaps bad people doing bad things, she slipped the rain slicker on. The storm had darkened the late-afternoon sky, so she grabbed a flashlight. Then she slipped the compact digital camera that was her constant companion while on the job into her coat pocket.

Before leaving the cottage, she also retrieved her weapon, holstering it at her waist. She clipped her badge next to the Glock.

Jason's words whispered through her mind. *The last thing any of us needs is you running around the island chasing danger like a dog chasing a cat. Eventually you'll catch a mouthful. And then what?*

She harrumphed. She could handle any trouble that came her way.

Promise me you're not going to do anything rash, Joe had said.

How many times had she heard that before? Investigating was in her blood, it was a part of her, like breathing.

Snatching up the rental car keys, she hurried out into the storm, turning her head to the side to keep the rain out of her eyes and the wind from whipping her ponytail into her face. Once she reached the road to town, the going was slow from the combination of others braving the elements and the hammering rain and whipping wind that threatened to tear the steering wheel out of her hand.

She drove as close to the Corrinda estate as the public roads would take her, hoping not to advertise her presence to anyone who might be watching, then parked on the shoulder of the road and left the car.

A gust of wind rattled the slicker and water falling in big chunky drops pelted her jean-clad legs. Tucking the flashlight into the waistband of her jeans, she cautiously walked down the estate drive, staying on the edge of the road so she could bail into the lush foliage in case anyone came along. She didn't want a repeat of what happened on the boat.

An intimidating wrought-iron gate with twisting metal prongs like an intricate spiderweb blocked further progress. An unmanned guardhouse stood to the side and an electronic keypad waited to be used by those with the combination.

Angie veered to the right and wiggled her way through the tall, prickly arborvitaes that grew in a row along the ten-foot-high metal fence running along the property line. She picked up a small rock and tossed it at the fence to test whether the fence was electrified. It wasn't. She blew out a relieved breath.

She looked at the house on the cliff and let out a silent whistle. No wonder the Corrindas' henchmen tooled around in a nice boat. And Chief Decker wouldn't mess with them. The outward display of wealth said the Corrindas could afford to buy loyalties.

Massive barely described the pale yellow structure that stretched out along the cliff's edge. Huge pillars flanked the double front doors. Beautifully crafted windows lined the front of the house. Angie guessed the inside would appear light and airy on sunny days. Several balconies with arched French doors jutted out along the upper portion of the house.

A magnificent thirty-foot-high trellis thick with jasmine covered the side of the home that faced Angie. The fragrant, white blossoms bowed their heads in the wind. Manicured hedges cut into interesting shapes lined the walkways. The landscaped yard reminded her of the English gardens so popular with the wealthy aristocrats of New England.

From the front all seemed quiet and still despite the storm raging around the house. Though she didn't see any security cameras, she didn't doubt that there were some. Thankful for the cover of the full arborvitaes, Angie continued along the property's edge and made her way toward the back, careful to keep low lest her movements were detected.

Up ahead the fence ended and the ground gave way to a craggy cliff facing the ocean. The blustery weather blowing up the face of jagged rocks buffeted her, making the rain pelt her face. The view of the wildly tossing waves stretching out as far as she could see took her breath away. No wonder the Corrindas had chosen this spot for their house.

Slowly, she made her way along the cliff's ragged edge until she had a full view of the cove below. From where she crouched, she couldn't see how anyone got down to the dock sheltered by the rocky walls of the cove.

Her gaze took in the back of the house, just as spectacular as the front, with more balconies and stunningly crafted windows. The large back patio, now battened down for the storm, featured curving lines all the way around the Olympic-size pool and butted against a stripe of grass that bordered the cliff's edge.

A small structure stood off to the side. Curiosity burned in her chest. Was there an elevator or a staircase that led to the cove? She thought better of exploring the building, which had to be secured with an alarm. Inching closer to the rim of the cliff, she hoped to glimpse some activity below.

An armed man patrolled the dock but otherwise all was quiet. Taking out her camera, she flipped the flash button to off so as to not announce her position, then snapped a couple of shots. The sky had darkened considerably. She wasn't sure any images would show up. But at least she was doing something productive.

On her left a twig snapped. Her gaze jerked toward the sound. Nothing there. Obviously, she was more stressed by this venture than she'd realized. Still, she sent up a silent prayer. *Lord, please watch over me.*

Suddenly a hand clamped over her mouth, not quite smothering an instinctual, startled yelp.

Frantic adrenaline burst through her system. She rolled left, trying to break her attacker's hold as her right hand went for her Glock.

Strong fingers clasped her wrist. "Stand down, Officer."

The harshly whispered command froze Angie in place. She blinked as a man came into view, so close she could smell mint and man mingled with the damp earth.

"Shh," he hissed. "I'm taking my hand away. Don't scream or you'll ruin everything."

She stared mutely as her mind recognized Jason, dressed in camouflage. Streaks of grease paint marred his handsome face.

She went limp with relief that was short-lived as the significance of his presence, not to mention his garb, rammed through her brain. Her gaze snagged on the long-lens camera encased in a protective clear plastic sheath slung around his neck and the semiautomatic at his hip.

"Who are you?" she whispered. "And this time, I want the truth."

FIVE

Blinking rainwater from his eyes, Jason ground his teeth. The truth could get them killed.

But he couldn't have her running around doing her own investigation. He hadn't expected her to take it this far. He'd underestimated her tenacity.

He contemplated how much to reveal. And decided just enough to satisfy her and make her back off, but not enough to destroy the cover he'd meticulously built.

"I'm ICE—Immigration and Customs Enforcement," he said. "Now do you understand why you need to back off?"

Her eyes widened as dawning entered the dark depths. "You're undercover. Okay, that makes sense. But you could have shared that with me a few days ago."

"I'm risking my life sharing anything, at any time."

He glanced around, feeling the pressing need to get her out of there. If she were seen… He didn't want to think what would happen. He couldn't allow anything bad to happen to her. He couldn't take another death on his conscience.

"Come on. Let's get you out of here," he said. "Follow me. And stay low."

He backed up to give her room to rise to a crouch. Taking her by the hand, he pulled her away from the cliff's edge and urged her toward safety along the arborvitaes. Gusts of air pushed at their backs. Rain made the ground soppy and dangerously slippery.

From the house to their right, a bright spotlight lit the backyard and a shout rang out above the sounds of the storm. "Halt! I'll shoot."

They both reacted by abandoning stealth for an all-out run. Panicked fear pumped through Jason as he yanked Angie forward so that his body protected her. He had a flak vest on. Angie didn't.

"Go, go," he urged. "Stay near the bushes. Keep your head low."

A loud bang raised the hairs on Jason's neck. Thunder? The thwack of a bullet hitting the trees sent his heart rate into overdrive. Not thunder, but a rifle.

Oh, dear Father in Heaven, not again. Please, not again.

Gale winds streaked through the air. Stinging rain fell from the sky. Men's shouts were barely discernible above the noises of the storm as Jason followed closely on Angie's heels. They left the cover of the arborvitaes and ran down the private drive, splashing through rivulets of rainwater. Behind them the sound of metal scraping across concrete heralded the opening of the gate. A fresh rush of adrenaline pumped through Jason.

"My car!" Angie shouted, pointing to where she'd parked her rental on the side of the road.

"Keys?" Jason asked, holding out his hand while he ran. He could barely believe they'd made it to the road unscathed. Obviously, the man with the gun wasn't a sharpshooter. A small blessing.

Without breaking stride, Angie dug the keys from her pocket, hit the unlock button and then tossed them in a high arc. He caught them and skidded to a halt beside the vehicle before flinging open the door and jumping inside.

Beside him, Angie dropped into the passenger seat. "Go, go!"

Jason started the engine and stomped on the gas. Cranking the wheel, he sent the car in a skidding U-turn. Through the rearview mirror, he saw two men with guns running down the drive and stopping as Jason and Angie roared out of reach.

Heart still pumping at a rapid clip, Jason hit the steering wheel with the heel of his hand as he drove faster than the speed limit toward Angie's cottage. He flipped on the headlights, twin beams of light illuminating the nightfall.

Fury seethed in his belly and crawled up his neck to burn his cheeks. "Do you have any idea how dangerous that was? You could have been killed if I hadn't found you first."

She punched him in the arm. Fuming fire lit up her dark eyes. "Hey, don't yell at me. If you hadn't snuck up on me I wouldn't have made any noise *and* I would have gotten out of there undetected."

"What if they come after you?"

"They didn't get a good look at our faces. There's no way anyone at the house could even ID us."

Even though he knew she was right he snorted and shook his head in exasperation. "You have to leave the island tonight."

"I'm not leaving," she said, a stubborn note in her voice echoing inside the car.

"Don't make me go over your head."

"What?"

"I'll talk to my superior, who will talk to yours."

"Ohhh, I'm scared." She sounded anything but. She heaved a sigh. "Look, I can help you. Just fill me in."

"No. This is a federal investigation and you're interfering. How would you like it if I came to your precinct and butted in?"

By the wry twist of her lips, he knew he'd made his point. He eased his foot off the gas and slowed to a more reasonable pace. The last thing he needed was to be pulled over. Dressed as he was, with grease paint obscuring his face, red flags would be raised sky high and questions would be asked.

He turned down the street leading to Angie's cottage. The whole street was unlit. No house lights, no streetlights. Obviously the power had gone out due to the wind and rain. He parked the rental as close to the front door as possible. Not that it really mattered; they were both soaking wet.

He followed Angie to the cottage's front porch overhang, where he stopped her from entering. The beam of his flashlight shined on a small folded note propped against her door.

In a flurry of movement, Angie turned the key in the lock, pushed the door open and dashed into the entryway, where she grabbed a large beach bag and dug around inside. She produced a pair of thin rubber gloves.

"You carry gloves in your beach bag?" Jason asked.

Clearly the detective had issues if she couldn't even pack for the beach without including work paraphernalia.

She shrugged. "You never know what you'll need."

She slipped the gloves over her hands and picked up the neatly folded piece of cream-colored vellum lying on the door's threshold. Her hands were steady as she unfolded the sheet. She tilted the paper toward the glow of the flashlight's beam. A small frown appeared between her dark arched eyebrows.

Jason moved to stand beside her so he could see the script written in bold strokes across the page.

An invitation for brunch the next day at the Corrinda estate.

Alarm slithered down his spine. "Uh, no," Jason stated before she even spoke. He didn't have to be a mind reader to know she'd want to go. "Don't even think about it. You are not accepting that invitation."

She lifted her determined gaze to meet his. "This could be your break in the case."

"I don't want it at your expense. It's too dangerous." The thought of sending her to a situation he couldn't control or at least predict the outcome of sent chills of apprehension sliding over his skin.

"I can handle the danger."

"You don't know what you could be walking into."

The electricity came back on with little fanfare. A table lamp glowed. He recognized the hum of the refrigerator and the beep of the microwave resetting itself.

Angie didn't miss a beat. "I can take care of myself. I am a cop, remember?"

"I remember. And you're tenacious and controlling and way out of your depth here."

Anger flitted across her pretty face. "Then fill me in. Do you know what the Corrindas are up to?"

He didn't. And wasn't sure how this family fit with Picard. His gut told him there was a connection, and until he figured it out, he wasn't going to allow Angie to forge ahead and put her life in jeopardy. For all he knew, this could be a trap to draw him out, in which case his cover was blown.

But why bait him with Angie? Why not just come after him directly? Unless—they weren't sure there was a federal involvement and his cover was still intact. Their invitation might not be about him at all.

But that didn't mean Angie wasn't in danger. As she'd pointed out, she was a cop. And a cop asking questions made people nervous. Especially if they had something to hide.

He'd have to get clearance from his SAC before he released any details to Angie. Protective instincts surged. If he revealed the situation to her, then she'd be in even more danger. He didn't want that. "Look, this isn't your fight. Go back to your life in Boston."

She rolled her eyes. "When are you going to realize that's not happening? I'm not leaving until I see this through. Either work with me, arrest me or stay out of my way."

She moved past him toward the kitchen, her shapely frame vibrating with excitement and strength, carrying the sheet of paper by the corner. She pulled out a sandwich-size plastic bag from a drawer, slipped the invitation inside and sealed the bag closed.

Frustration pounded at Jason's temple. He rubbed his tight jaw and immediately regretted doing so as the grease paint he'd used for camouflage coated his palm. Could this get any more complicated? "Look, you can't stay here. You need to at least move to a hotel."

"Not happening. The Corrindas don't know it was you or me at their place tonight. I'm sure news of my presence and my questions have reached their ears. It's a small island, remember. They sent the invitation to breakfast as a way to get me off their case. Nothing more." She put the bagged evidence in a drawer. "Speaking of food, I'm starved. Would you like some leftover lasagna? I had some delivered and they brought enough for six people."

Across the divide of the kitchen counter, he met

her direct gaze. "You really aren't going to listen to me, are you?"

She smiled sweetly. "I'll listen if you tell me something worth listening to."

She was so cute, and smart and sassy standing there with those big, beautiful brown eyes staring at him with challenge, dripping ponytail and soaked clothes. She had to feel as clammy as he did. "I should go change," he said gruffly.

What he wanted to do was close the space between them and kiss her. Not a good idea. Not at all. A romantic relationship with her was not on his agenda. Getting emotionally involved would only lead to disappointment and heartache. For them both. He had no intention of leading her on with promises he wouldn't keep. He'd learned his lesson with Serena.

Her lips twisted in a wry grimace. "Me, too. How about you come back in an hour and we can discuss how to play this in the morning."

"You're assuming I'm suddenly okay with you accepting the Corrindas' invitation?"

She walked around the counter toward him and stopped inches away to stare him down. A cop move. She was tall for a woman, almost matching his six-foot frame. He liked that he could look directly into her eyes. If she'd meant to intimidate, she'd veered way off base. So much for the cop move. Those pretty, mocha orbs lured him in, making him yearn for something he'd already decided was off-limits.

"I think once you realize the opportunity knocking

here, you'll agree that the best thing would be for us to collaborate. I can be your eyes and ears," she said and pinned him with a meaningful look. "Providing I know what's at stake."

Shaking his head, he grabbed hold of his hormones and stepped back. A small laugh escaped him. "You really are something. Let me see what I can do. I'll be back in an hour. Can I use your car? I left my truck a mile down the road from the Corrindas' estate."

"Should we go get it now?"

"No. I'll retrieve it in the morning."

She swiped the keys from the end table where she'd dropped them. "Here."

"Thanks. Lock the door behind me."

She gave him a droll look. "Like I wouldn't?"

"Right." He slipped out the door and hurried to the car. As he started the engine, he wondered at the wisdom of involving her. But she was right. This could be the big break in the case he'd been waiting for. He mustn't ever forget his objective. Find and capture Picard. No matter the cost.

He only hoped Angie wouldn't be the one to pay the price.

Angie allowed the hot shower to wash away the adrenaline and lingering fear of the past few hours. She'd been shot at, sneaked up on, and Jason wasn't who he claimed to be.

That was enough to blow anyone's mind.

She should have guessed Jason was some type of

Fed. ICE, to be exact. OI—Office of Investigations? Probably, if he was undercover. *A charter-boat captain.* Ha! Was Jason Bodewell even his real name? Unlikely.

His unpredictable behavior now made so much more sense. Obviously, he'd been using her and what she'd seen to further his own agenda, whatever that may be. She could only hope he'd realize working together would be a benefit.

Excitement trilled through her. She could help in a federal investigation. She'd never doubted her choice to become a homicide detective, but she liked to keep her options open.

She changed into dry sweatpants and a long-sleeved T-shirt, combed out her curls, which loved the humidity, and used the blow-dryer just enough to keep the ends from dripping water on her clean clothes. She started to gather the mass to pull back, then decided to let the long curls bounce around her shoulders. Most evenings she kept her hair down, giving her scalp a break from the heavy ponytail.

Trying to ignore the nervous jitters reminding her that Jason would soon return, she puttered in the kitchen. Outside the storm raged. Branches scratched at the siding, rain tapped at the windows and an occasional clap of thunder made her jump as she set the table while the leftover Italian food heated in the oven. She made a salad and buttered some bread to warm at the last minute.

A knock sounded at the door. Her pulse bounced. Not taking anything for granted, she put her hand on the holstered weapon at her waist and moved to the door. She peered through the peephole. The soft glow of the porch light haloed Jason's clean and freshly shaved face beneath the hood of his slicker.

She opened the door and admitted him. "Hi. Here, let me take your jacket."

Unmoving, he stared at her a moment.

Feeling suddenly self-conscious, she asked, "Is something wrong?"

Shaking his head, his lips tipped upward at the corners. "Not at all. I really like your hair down. You have beautiful hair."

Both touched and pleased by the compliment, she inclined her head. "Thank you."

He slipped out of the slicker and hung it by the hood on the standing coat rack in the entryway. He'd changed into soft-looking chinos showing the smattering of rain that had obviously pelted him when he'd been exposed to the elements. His Henley-style long-sleeved shirt was a shade of blue that matched his eye color exactly and stretched over taut muscles. She smothered a sigh of pleasure.

"Hmm, something smells good," he said.

"It is good. Have you eaten at Fiona's?" she asked as she preceded him to the kitchen.

"Oh, yeah. One of the island's best."

"Sit. Let me serve you," she said when he entered the kitchen.

"I'd rather help," he countered and stuck his hand in a pot holder. "Is the lasagna ready to come out?"

"I'm sure it is," she said, watching him take the pan of lasagna from the oven and move it to the stovetop. She liked that he wanted to help and that he didn't just expect to be catered to.

"Serving spoon?"

She pointed to a drawer next to the stove.

She took the salad to the table and then returned to pop the bread in the still-hot oven. "This will just take a minute or two."

"I'll dish us up some lasagna," he said and reached for the two plates sitting on the counter.

This companionable ease with which they moved around the kitchen felt at turns odd and yet so right. She didn't entertain much at her apartment, preferring to dine out on dates. It was much easier to control the situation in a public venue.

Allowing anyone into her private world wasn't something she did easily or often. She'd learned the hard way that men were either turned off or intimidated by her career or wanted to conquer her to build up their own egos.

She'd really like to find a guy who was comfortable in his own skin and comfortable letting her be herself. She eyed Jason speculatively. Could he be that guy? Definitely worth considering.

They sat to eat. She hesitated a moment. Normally, she liked to pray before partaking of her meals. Would Jason mind?

"Is something wrong?" he asked.

"No," she said quickly, unsure how to ask if he'd

be okay with her saying a blessing over their food. She could always say it silently. God would hear her.

"Would you like for me to say grace?"

Surprised, she beamed. "Please do."

His clear blue eyes twinkled before he bowed his head. Angie followed suit, but she struggled to keep her gaze off his face. She doubted this man humbled himself much to anyone. But knowing he did before the Lord warmed her from the inside out.

"Dear Lord, thank you for this food you've provided. Please bless it to our bodies. I ask that you would watch over us as we move forward in our endeavors. Amen."

"Amen," she murmured, liking his simple yet straightforward prayer. She picked up the salad tongs. "May I?"

He held out his plate. "Please."

She grinned at how their formality contrasted with their encounter behind the Corrinda estate. "How did you know I'd want to pray?"

His gaze flicked to her neck. "I noticed the cross you wear."

The tiny gold symbol of her faith lay against her skin beneath her T-shirt, the light pressure comforting. "Have you been a believer your whole life?"

He dropped his gaze and concentrated on his plate. "Yes." He took a bite of food, preventing him from answering further.

When he didn't elaborate, she decided not to press. One's faith was a personal journey to be respected.

Obviously, he wanted to keep that part of himself private. But why did the fact that he didn't want to open up and talk about his faith sting?

Pushing away the unsettling thought, she changed the subject by asking, "Did you talk to your SAC?"

Wiping his mouth with a napkin, he nodded. "I have permission to fill you in. But, just so you know, your superior isn't too happy."

She grimaced. "I'll bet. Taking a vacation hadn't exactly been my idea. My boss had practically demanded I use my accumulated vacation time before I lost it."

"Why doesn't that surprise me?" he teased.

She made a face. She couldn't help that she was a workaholic. And the timing of her forced vacation had come just after her detective partner had announced his engagement to heiress Kristina Worthington.

Angie had had a secret crush on Gabe since the day they'd been partnered. But acting on her feelings would have been disastrous because he'd never been anything other than professional with her. Thankfully, Gabe never knew she'd had feelings for him. At least, she hoped he didn't know. How embarrassing.

"What are you thinking about?" Jason peered at her intently.

Heat touched her cheeks, but she kept her gaze steady. *Never show weakness,* her father was always telling her brothers.

A sentiment that Angie had adopted as well, whether Dad had intended her to do so or not. "Nothing worth mentioning."

His gaze narrowed. "Something that makes you sad."

"I'm not sad." She hated how easily he read her.

He arched an eyebrow, challenging her statement.

"Shouldn't you be filling me in on your assignment?"

A knowing smile played at the corners of his well-shaped mouth. Obviously he was well aware she'd used the question to divert the subject. "Yes."

He sat back, settling in to tell his tale. "About a year ago we had intel that an illegal arms dealer was working out of New Mexico, shipping contraband through Mexico to the Middle East. The Mexican government had found the connection in their country and asked the U.S. to take care of the problem on our end. We tracked the dealer, a man named Felix Picard, to a villa outside Anapra.

"Only problem was, Picard had somehow been tipped off. He was gone." Jason's lips twisted with bitterness and a haunted expression entered his eyes. "A good man lost his life that night."

Angie sensed Jason's pain as he'd sensed hers just moments ago. She reached across the table to lay her hand over his clenched fist. "Someone you were close to."

He nodded. "My partner, Garrett. We'd gone to high school together. Joined the military together and then ICE."

Her heart ached with sympathy. "I'm so sorry."

He met her gaze. "He shouldn't have died. And when I find Picard, I'll make the man pay."

Angie frowned, not liking the note of vicious hatred behind his words. "You'll bring the man to justice, you mean."

One side of Jason's mouth lifted in a near snarl. "Yeah. Justice."

Up until that moment she hadn't understood why she was there, but now she did. God had sent her to Loribel because Jason really did need her. Needed her to make sure he didn't do something foolish, like the premeditated murder of Picard.

"You think this guy is here on the island? What is the connection to the Corrinda family?"

He blinked, his expression clearing, returning to the man she'd come to know over the past few days. "Yes to the first question and don't know yet to the second."

"Do you have a photo of Picard? Maybe I've seen him."

Jason heaved a beleaguered sigh. "That's the problem." He ran his hands through his hair in obvious frustration. "See, Picard doesn't exist. At least not in any database on this planet. There's no birth record, no social security number, no driver's license. The man's a phantom."

"Then how do you know he's even real?"

"He's real, all right. We've captured men in his employ who have led the authorities to various places where he has stashed weapons. But no one can give a consistent description. Some say he's albino, others say dark and sinister. Obviously Picard uses disguises.

He could be anyone. And for now the government is content to let him stay under the radar."

Flabbergasted by that tidbit, she said, "Even though he killed an agent?"

Derision scored his face. "Yeah."

"Then how can you be here?"

"My boss isn't so forgiving as the mucky-mucks on Capitol Hill."

A shiver of trepidation chased up Angie's spine. "And how do you know he's on Loribel?"

"We've intercepted a shipment of rocket launchers coming out of these waters. They had Picard's stamp on them."

"Stamp?"

"Yeah, he's arrogant enough to put a distinctive stamp in the shape of a capital *P* with an ivy vine and a snake intertwined around the letter."

"Creepy. Could he be using the Corrinda family as cover? That would make sense given the prime location of the cove." Nervous anticipation twitched in her stomach. Did she really want to accept the invitation?

"Possibly." He sat forward, his blue eyes darkening with concern. "Look, you don't have to do this. I could get you off the island tonight."

She bolstered her courage and her resolve. *Show no weakness*. "No. I'm doing this."

He stared at her for a long moment before nodding. "Okay, then. In the morning, you'll come to my place and I'll prep you."

"Prep me?"

"You don't think I'd let you go in there alone, do you? You'll have a wire and a video feed."

"They might anticipate a wire."

"Trust me. Even if they suspect, they won't find my state-of-the-art equipment."

Her heart skipped a beat. What was that adage? *Be careful what you wish for.*

Now she understood how true those words were.

SIX

The next morning, the sky was overcast, the wind had retreated and the rain had ceased. Angie arrived at Jason's condo per the directions he'd written out the night before since she doubted she'd be able to find it again after she'd dropped him off. The condo complex sprawled over prime beach property adjacent to the marina and was very appealing in the light of day. Probably once landscaped walks led through the center court to Building C, but Angie had to step through scattered bits and pieces of flowers and bushes cluttering the way. A reminder of yesterday's raging storm.

The central common area of the condo complex needed a bit of cleanup, too, Angie mused. Broken palm fronds lay atop of the round metal tabletops positioned around a concrete patio lined with cold barbecue grills.

She found Unit Ten at the far end of the building facing inland. But Jason hadn't moved here for the view. Taking a steadying breath, she knocked. A nervous flutter made the banana she'd eaten for breakfast tumble in her stomach. Because of what the day might bring during her meeting with the Corrindas or because she was about to see Jason again?

She honestly didn't know.

The door opened to reveal Jason, looking attractive in khaki, pleat-front pants and a navy blue pullover shirt. He had on an empty shoulder holster, also. Gone was the laid-back yachtsman. Jason was all business now. "Good morning. You're right on time."

"Morning," she replied and stepped inside.

He gave her an approving once-over. "Perfect."

He meant her work outfit, right? She tugged self-consciously on her tailored suit jacket, which she'd been wearing when she arrived on Loribel. She'd chosen her traditional pantsuit and collared button-down blouse because it was professional, yet the lines did a lot for her figure.

The scent of rich coffee permeated the air, offering distraction. "Hmm. That smells good. Can I have a cup?"

"Of course." He headed toward the open L-shaped kitchen with blond cabinets and stainless-steel appliances.

Angie glanced around, automatically cataloging the room. A desk in the corner with a laptop open and running. Nearby sat a glass-top dining table and four chairs covered in a bold striped material. A hallway led off to the left and had three closed doors. Two bedrooms, she assumed, and a bath.

She wasn't sure what she'd expected, but the contrasts between soothing beiges and splashes of color piqued her interest. He wasn't a utilitarian type or messy.

The walls and carpet were a soft cream broken by a dark red sectional with multicolored throw pillows strewn over its surface. A big-screen television, much like the one her eldest brother had given her parents for Christmas, served as the focal point near the sliding-glass doors, which led to a small terrace. Colorful abstract prints graced the walls, pulling the colors of the couch and the creams together.

Various pieces of electronic equipment lay scattered over the surface of the square coffee table in front of the couch.

She arched an eyebrow. "Is all that for me?"

Jason laughed as he handed her a steaming mug of coffee. "Not *all* of it. Come sit down."

Holding the mug with both hands and inhaling the aromatic perfume of the rich coffee, Angie followed him to the couch and sat beside him, vividly aware of the energy coming from him. "So what does a super-secret ICE agent have in his grab bag?"

He picked up a small disc about the size of a quarter. "This is a tracking device. Can I have your shoe?"

She slipped off one of the soft-soled Mary Jane shoes as an uneasy feeling rose in the pit of her stomach. "Why do I need tracking?"

"You can't be too careful."

He was thorough, she'd give him that.

He took out the insole of the shoe and placed the round disc inside and then replaced the insole before handing the shoe back to her. "I don't think we'll need it, but—"

"Just in case," she finished for him, not even wanting to contemplate a scenario where the tracking device would be needed. But knowing he'd have her back gave her a big dose of comfort.

He dug through a small box. "This is a button camera with audio feed." He held up a small unit that did indeed look like a navy button on the front, with matching coated wiring on the back and a short dark cable dangling down. "May I have your coat?"

Setting her coffee down on the table, she shrugged out of her navy suit jacket. He cut off the top button and replaced it with the button camera, hiding the cable beneath the lapel of the coat. He held the garment up for inspection. She couldn't tell the difference between the buttons. Impressive. "This won't set off any alarms if they wand you."

He referred to a handheld metal detector. "I should probably leave my Glock with you then, too," she said.

"Probably wise."

She slipped her holster and weapon from her waistband and handed them over. Jason clipped the holster to his own waistband. Angie felt naked without her piece.

From another small box Jason took out something that looked like a flesh-toned piece of wax. "An earpiece. You'll be able to hear me."

"I've used these before. You've thought of everything," she commented as she took the device from him. Their fingers brushed, sending small little shivers up her arm. How could such a simple touch affect her so? It didn't make sense.

She put the piece in her ear, wiggling it around to get it comfortable. He inspected her ear, his face close. If she turned her head, their lips would meet. She held herself still even as the urge to turn toward him gripped her in an iron fist. The last thing she needed was to make a mess of the situation by acting like a love-crazed teen. When he moved back, she let out a breath she hadn't realized she'd held.

"Looks good," he said and handed her back her coat. "Are you ready?"

"You bet." As ready as she'd ever be considering she was going in wired. Investigation was her forte, not acting. But she could do this. She was sure of it.

Jason picked up a handheld device a little bigger than a PDA that blipped a red dot. He held it out for her view. "That red dot is you."

Then he clicked a button and turned the screen for her to see. The image on the handheld was of the room from the angle of the button camera. "I can monitor you from anywhere."

"Cool," she said.

"The latest and greatest of techno wonders." He picked up a briefcase, cleared a spot on the table and then opened the lid to reveal two semiauto weapons and several clips of ammo. He armed himself, placing one loaded gun in the shoulder holster and the other in an ankle holster. He dropped a clip into each front pocket. "We're good to go."

After grabbing a black rain slicker from the hall closet, Jason led the way back to Angie's car. He put another small tracking device beneath the front passenger wheel well. As she slid into the driver's side, he opened the back and climbed in.

"What are you doing?" She turned in her seat to stare at him. "You're not coming with me."

He grinned. "Just drive. When we get close to the gate I'll get out."

Feeling queasy with nervous anticipation, she nodded and started the engine. Aware of Jason in the backseat, his heated gaze warming her cheeks, Angie tried to concentrate on the road, weaving around debris and pedestrians. Ten minutes later, when she reached the place where she'd parked yesterday, she pulled over.

Jason laid a hand on her shoulder, the pressure reassuring and warm. "Be careful. If you feel threatened or in any danger, just say *time out* and I'll come in after you."

Somehow she didn't doubt that he would come to her rescue if she needed it. She dipped her chin until she touched the back of his hand. "Thanks."

She could handle this. She'd handled worse. Entering the privileged world of the Corrinda family would be a walk in the park compared to some of the gang-infested housing projects she'd had to deal with in the past.

But she also knew overconfidence could get her killed.

Out of habit, she reached toward her hip to touch her Glock, needing the security its presence brought. Not there. It was securely fastened at Jason's waist. She suppressed a shiver.

Dear Lord, please watch over me. Protect me.

Jason slipped out of the car and she drove the rest of the way to the gate. In the light of day, the massive wrought-iron structure framed by the dark storm clouds still present in the sky created a gothic picture that sent a chill skating over her skin.

The small guardhouse was still unmanned, so she rolled down the window and pushed the red button on the keypad, hoping that was the correct way to announce her arrival.

A male voice asked for her name. She gave it and then a second later the large gate creaked open, the metal scraping across the paved road adding to the spooky feel. Beyond the gate, the stunning house came into view as she drove forward to park near brick steps leading to the front door.

She got out of the car and stared up at the large mansion. Pristine and well kept. Many windows with balconies and sheer curtains blocking the interior view.

What secrets did this house hold? She'd soon find out.

As she approached the enormous wood front door, it swung open. A tall older man wearing a dark suit and white dress shirt stood waiting, his aged face pressed into unsmiling repose. "Detective Carlucci, come in. You are awaited in the dining hall."

"Thank you." No wand or pat down. She let out a little relieved breath. Her surveillance equipment would go undetected.

She followed her greeter through the elaborate entryway with its wide staircase and gleaming wood floors, through a set of French doors to a large dining room. Which indeed looked like a long hall. An extended table set for lunch dominated the center of the room.

Both of the end seats were occupied and in the middle were four chairs. Three of which were also occupied by two identical men and a woman.

Angie blinked back surprise. She hadn't expected to see one man in particular.

In her ear, Jason said, *"What is he doing there? Angle a little to the left so I can get a better view."*

Accommodating the request, Angie shifted to give the button camera a better view of the whole table.

"Better."

The elderly man who sat at the head of the table rose and, leaning heavily on a cane, shuffled forward to take her hand. His linen shirt and slacks hung from his thin body. His gnarled fingers were calloused and rough against her skin. Dark, probing eyes stared at her from an olive-toned face, wrinkled from the passage of time. "My dear, let me introduce myself, Horatio Corrinda. So glad you could join us today. I understand you've been asking about our family."

No secrets in this town. Angie tilted her head in acknowledgment. "Nice to meet you, sir."

"I hope we can answer any questions you may have," Horatio said.

Jason's voice echoed in her head. *"Where's Picard? That's the question."*

Hoping her face didn't reveal anything but politeness, Angie said, "Thank you. I appreciate your kindness."

"These are my grandsons. Erik and Edmund." He swept a hand toward the handsome twin men. They were in their mid-thirties and had hair the color of sand and wore finely cut power suits. They nodded in unison.

"Tweedle Dee and Tweedle Dum. What are they doing here?"

Forcing herself to ignore Jason, Angie smiled a greeting, which wasn't returned by either man. "Do you reside here, as well?"

Edmund answered, his voice cold, "No. We're just visiting."

Erik said in a more congenial tone, "I live full-time in Berlin. I understand you're from Boston. And law enforcement is a family affair."

"They've done their homework."

"I am," Angie replied.

Horatio moved to stand beside the woman still seated at the table. "My wife, Karla."

They made a handsome couple. Angie moved forward to offer her hand to the older woman. "Nice to meet you."

Karla inclined her head in a regal acknowledgment

as she briefly took Angie's hand. She had fading blond hair swept up in a top knot and fine porcelain features gently lined with age. The chiffon outfit she wore reminded Angie of the retro sixties outfits so popular in magazines. The woman had to have been stunning in her youth.

"And of course, you know our other guest," Horatio said with just a trace of amusement in his voice.

"Only too well. Now we know for sure he's on the Corrindas' payroll."

Angie kept her expression neutral as she greeted the man directly across the table. "Chief Decker, interesting surprise."

Decker gave her a tight thinning of his lips in a semblance of a smile. "Mr. Corrinda asked me to join you all this morning because he wasn't sure of your intentions. Nor is your boss."

She blinked. He'd spoken to Chief McDaniel? Before or after ICE contacted him?

"Cheap shot calling her boss, Decker, but not a hit."

Angie hid a smile at Jason's words. To Decker she said, "My intentions are the same as they were when I came into your office a few days ago."

His eyes hardened. "You're not on duty, Officer. I will not have you running around my island upsetting the citizens with your accusations and innuendos. You are on vacation, Detective. I suggest you act like it."

She'd struck a nerve, huh? What was the police

chief's story? "I haven't accused anyone of anything nor have I alluded to anything other than what I've witnessed."

She was sure Decker had already told the Corrindas everything, but to be sure, she turned to Horatio. "Did Chief Decker tell you I saw a body bag being dumped in the ocean? Did he explain to you that a boat that I was in was stopped and boarded by armed men in a boat that now is moored in your cove? Did he also tell you that those same men chased me away from the cove?"

"Ohhhh, the subtle approach. That's the way to lay it all out there. Gustsy but risky. Just say the word, and I'm there."

With Jason talking in her ear, Angie barely heard Karla's small gasp while the twins exchanged a glance that Angie couldn't read.

Horatio's bushy silver eyebrows rose nearly to his thinning gray hairline. "Body?"

Obviously Decker hadn't shared everything. Interesting.

Horatio turned to peer at Decker. "What is this about a body?"

Red faced, the chief said, "There was no body. I searched the area extensively and found—" he gave Angie a pointed, hard glare "—nothing."

Angie focused on Horatio. "What about the armed men in the cove? Are they in your employ?"

Edmund spoke up. "Of course they are. We employ a small army of highly trained and highly legal security experts. You would not believe the type of people who would like nothing better than to bring my grandfather and his empire down."

"Yeah, right. Or maybe the old man is Picard. Or maybe one of the grandsons?"

Angie tried to concentrate on the conversation with the people in front of her rather than the one in her ear. "So each of the men in your employ are licensed to carry?"

"Yes," Edmund said.

"The guns I saw weren't legal weapons. How do you explain that?" she asked.

Erik frowned. "I'll bring that up with the head of our security team."

"Who would that be?"

"Who would that be?" Angie repeated Jason's question.

"Enrique Morsi," Edmund said. "He came highly recommended."

"Good job, Angie."

Jason's approval warmed her.

"Please, please," Karla finally spoke, her velvety voice soft yet commanding. "This talk of guns and security is upsetting. We invited the detective here for lunch. Please, everyone, sit."

"Quite right. Please, Detective Carlucci, have a seat," Horatio invited and motioned for Erik to pull out her chair. "When our meal is finished, the boys will give you any and all information you require to appease your sense of duty."

"*Well, well. How accommodating.*"

"Thank you." She hesitated before sitting. "Would you mind if I freshen up before we eat?"

"Of course," Karla said and waved a hand toward the butler who hovered near the edge of the door. "Fred, please show the detective to the powder room."

"Right this way," Fred said with a stately bow.

"*What are you doing?*"

Angie ignored the question as she followed Fred down the hall, through the entryway and down another long hall. Her gaze searched the ceiling corners and fixtures for hidden cameras. She didn't detect any.

Though she passed several closed doors, a set of closed double doors intrigued her. The den?

At the powder room, she waited for Fred to disappear from view back down the hall before she headed back to the double doors.

"*What are you doing? Angie, you're going to be caught. Don't go in there.*"

"Shh," she hissed as she pushed open the doors. The room indeed was an office, with large picture windows overlooking the side yard. In front of the windows stood a large cherry-wood desk and leather captain's chair. She closed the door behind her and hurried to the desk.

"*WHAT are you doing?*"

Flinching at the loudness of his voice, she said, "Looking. And stop talking so much. You're bugging me."

"*You're going to get yourself killed.*"

"Nonsense," she replied and took a tissue from the square box sitting on the corner. Using the tissue to keep from leaving fingerprints, she opened drawers. She wasn't sure what she was looking for. Something to make sense of the body bag and the illegal weapons.

"Well, if you're going to do this, then at least make sure the camera is recording the contents of the drawers and the desk. What's that beneath the file folder?"

She abandoned the drawer to move aside the file folder labeled Sanchez/Rodriquez lying on top of the desk. "A desk calendar."

She skimmed her finger over the dates. On the day she'd seen the body bag dump there was a notation, "blasters p/u."

"What do you think this means?"

"I don't know. Pick up the file again. Flip through it." She slowly did as asked, to allow the camera to record the content. From what she could tell, they were photocopies of old handwritten pages, perhaps from a journal. Why did Jason want to have a record of them?

"You better get back."

"You're right." She laid the folder down. Another notation on the calendar caught her attention but she didn't take the time to ponder its meaning. She had to get back. They would be wondering what was taking her so long.

Heart pounding, she cautiously opened the study

door and peered out. The hall was clear. She slipped out of the room and shut the door just as Fred rounded the corner.

"Ah, there you are. Mr. Corrinda was becoming worried," Fred intoned with dripping censure.

"Thank you, Fred," Angie said with a smile and glided past him. Just before entering the dining hall, she whispered to Jason, "Now you be quiet."

"Ma'am?" Fred said as he reached past her to open the door.

"It's so quiet here. I can hardly hear the ocean," she said quickly to cover herself.

"Yes, ma'am," he said.

Angie rejoined the Corrindas and noticed that Decker's seat was empty. Her face must have shown her surprise.

"Samuel had to get back to work," Karla said, her gaze demure, and yet there was a calculating shimmer in the green depths.

Without commenting, Angie took her seat, thanking Erik, who'd jumped up to pull out her chair.

A small cart laden with plates of fruit and pastries had been wheeled beside the dining table. As soon as she sat a plate was set in front of her filled with delicious-smelling eggs Benedict.

The conversation while they ate was congenial, with Mr. Corrinda regaling them with stories of his great-great-grandfather founding the island and the town of Loribel.

"Where did the name *Loribel* come from?" Angie

asked as she settled back, her appetite more than satisfied even if her professional curiosity wasn't.

"Named after my great-great-grandfather's ship, the *Loribel*. You see, Sanchez Corrinda was captain of the *Loribel* flying under the Spanish flag and carrying the dowry of a English noblewoman to her betrothed, a Spanish prince. When the waters turned bad, Sanchez made to anchor in the New World to await the storm, only to be attacked by the pirate Rodriquez."

"Aha. I knew that name sounded familiar."

Angie leaned her elbow on the arm of her chair and put her hand near her ear, wishing she could keep Jason from commenting. "And what happened to the *Loribel?*"

Erik said, "There are some who say that Rodriquez sank the *Loribel* and took the dowry to the Caribbean, where he wasted the gold on wine and women."

"Ah, that's what everyone thinks," Horatio said with a gleam in his eyes.

"You don't believe he did?" Angie asked.

"I know he didn't. Rodriquez died a poor man, all right. Not because he spent the treasure. As I said, the weather had turned bad. The *Loribel* did sink, but Rodriquez sailed away empty-handed because my great-great-grandfather managed to escape with the dowry and washed up on the shores of this island. For hundreds of years my ancestors have searched Loribel Island looking for the treasure Sanchez buried."

"Interesting story, but irrelevant."

"How do you know this?" Angie asked, the handwritten pages flashing in her mind. She couldn't wait to see what they said.

"The story was passed down through the generations. My great-great-grandfather couldn't read or write but he made sure his children could. On his deathbed, he dictated his life's story to his youngest son."

"Can we get back to the matter at hand? Guns? Picard?"

"I'm very interested in this story," Angie answered Jason aloud. "It sounds like the premise for a movie."

Horatio snorted. "Where do you think the Hollywood types got the idea?"

Angie smiled and found herself enjoying this old man. "Was the island populated when Sanchez landed here?"

His eyes twinkled. "Yes. There was a Native American tribe living on the island. Sanchez married one of the tribe's princesses. He used the dowry to claim the land and founded the town. He then buried the rest of the treasure in fear that Rodriquez would come back looking for it."

Remembering the tunnel she'd seen in the side of the cliffs, she asked, "Did Sanchez tell his son where he'd buried the treasure?"

Horatio gave a beleaguered sigh. "Unfortunately, no." Then he brightened and gave his grandsons a sidelong glance. "But we think we may know where it is, though." From the breast pocket of his linen shirt he produced a round gold coin and offered it for her inspection. "We found this in the side of the hill."

Taking the coin, she marveled at the piece of history in her hand. "This is real?"

"Yes, we've had it authenticated." He took the coin back and redeposited it into his pocket.

"So you're hunting treasure," she stated.

"That's why the armed security. They think the treasure is in the cove. This has nothing to do with Picard."

Palpable disappointment echoed in Jason's voice. Sympathy twisted around Angie's insides like the jasmine winding around the trellises on the outside of the Corrindas' house. She understood how much Jason wanted to find the gunrunner and bring him to justice. Though the look in his eyes and the note of hate in his voice when he'd talked of Picard made Angie almost glad they hadn't found the man.

She really didn't want to see Jason do something that could ruin his life.

SEVEN

A deluge of rain fell as Angie left the Corrinda estate. She was no closer to finding Picard than before. But at least now she understood why the Corrindas had an army of armed men and their purpose. To guard the site where Horatio and his grandsons believed the treasure to be hidden.

But the question remained, what had been in that black bag that she'd seen dumped in the ocean? If not a body, then what?

Up ahead, Jason emerged from the tree line, now wearing the rain slicker with the hood pulled over his face. She pulled the car to the side of the road and he climbed in. Rainwater dripped onto the seat.

"That was a complete waste of time," he stated glumly.

She peeled the earpiece from her ear and slipped into the pocket of her jacket. "So you didn't find Picard yet. If he's here on the island, you will."

Angie drove on toward his condo.

"Yeah, from your lips to God's ears," he said.

She slanted him a glance. "Have you prayed about it?"

He lifted one eyebrow. "Every day for the past six months. I don't think God is listening."

"Just because you haven't received an answer doesn't mean He's not listening." She slowed at a stop sign and turned to face him fully. "You know there's a Bible verse that talks about time from God's perspective."

Amusement danced in his gaze. "Really?"

"Yes, really. It basically says that to God, a day is a thousand years, and a thousand years is a day. I think the point being, time, as we humans understand the concept, is irrelevant. God moves when He deems the time to be right and always to our benefit."

"You sound as if you really believe that," he said, peering at her with curiosity in his eyes.

Sadness for his obvious doubts about her faith— and, she suspected, about his own—flooded her. She tried for some levity as she eased the car through an intersection. "What? You think I'm just giving you lip service? Of course I believe it."

He turned to stare out the window. "I wish I could be so sure. Garrett had faith like yours."

The pain in his voice packed a wallop. He was still taking his friend's death hard. Angie reached out a hand to touch his shoulder. "Faith isn't so hard. It's really coming to terms with our own inability to control life and knowing, believing, there is a loving God who can control everything."

He looked back at her and took her hand in his. "I'll try to remember that."

Warmth from his skin sent ribbons of heat up her arm to burn in her cheeks. Forcing herself to concentrate on driving with one hand, she turned the car into the parking lot of Jason's condo and halted in a space near the walkway.

He gave her hand a squeeze. "Come up. We can look at the pictures from Corrinda's office. At least the treasure story is a bit interesting."

She nodded. He released her and climbed out. She followed him to his condo. Once inside, he removed the button camera from her jacket. Then he hooked up the handheld device he'd been using to a USB cable attached to his laptop. Within moments, they were watching video of her visit with the Corrindas.

When they reached the part where she'd entered the office, he slowed the frames down. The first desk drawer was uninteresting, filled with normal office stuff: pens, stapler, scissors. The other two drawers were deeper and filled with hanging file folders.

The desk calendar came into view. "What do you think the notation about the blasters means?" Angie asked, staring at the screen. "And it's on the date I saw that boat dump what I still believe was a body bag."

"I believe you saw a body bag, but like I said before, I'm doubtful there was a *body* in it. No way would a boatload of men chase us away from a dead body. More likely drugs, guns or even explosives considering the work being done in the cove's tunnel."

She frowned, not liking the eerie sensation stealing over her. "That was an awfully big and heavy bag."

"Enough C-4 to blow the whole island to kingdom come."

"Or at the very least a big hole in the side of the cliff. But how can they be using explosives without anyone noticing?"

"If they timed their blast to coincide with the storm, anyone who heard the boom would just assume the noise was thunder."

"I'm not liking this," she said. A bad feeling rooted itself in the pit of her stomach. What if something went wrong and the Corridinas brought the whole side of the cliff down on themselves? What a rescue nightmare that would be.

On the computer screen, the images of Horatio Corrinda's journal entries appeared on the computer screen. Jason stilled each page and printed them.

He was about to shut the video off when Angie said, "Wait. Look at this." She pointed to the screen, her finger over the desktop calendar.

Jason highlighted the area and enlarged the view. The word *Mabuto* and a time written in bold strokes appeared on a dated square.

"Mabuto," Angie read aloud. "What do you think it means?"

When Jason didn't reply she turned to find him staring transfixed at the screen. "Sounds like a Congolese name." He turned to pin her with an excited look. "My gut tells me something is going down at the cove in two days. And we're going to be there."

Two days later, after careful planning and consulting a topographical map, Angie and Jason set out by boat to scout the best position for the surveillance of the Corrindas' private cove via the ocean and the beach to the west of the rock barrier. Unfortunately, the weather also decided not to play nice by brewing another tropical storm and threatening to turn into a full-blown hurricane. Jason quelled any nervousness about the weather. The mission was a go no matter what.

But he'd given Angie another chance to bail before they left the marina. She'd declined.

Despite the increasingly choppy water, Jason maneuvered the *Regina Lee* over the ocean to a short dock along a stretch of beach meant to be used by day picnickers. The Corrindas' private cove wasn't visible from the dock since the protruding land formation of rocks and foliage made a neat blockade. He cut the engine and coasted toward the wooden dock.

Angie stood beside him beneath the canopy over the helm, which provided little shelter from the slanting rain and whipping wind. He wore a waterproof, camouflage rain suit and had provided Angie a matching one. It clung to her in the wind, the green-and-brown-patterned hood revealing only the white oval of her face and her wide eyes and ruby cheeks.

"I'm going to jump onto the dock. I'll need you

to throw me the rope," he said. He moved to the side of the boat.

Just then a big swell lifted the boat. Angie stumbled into his arms. For a moment they stood toe to toe, her big brown eyes liquid pools he'd gladly drown in.

All around them the waves crashed. The boat bobbed and the wind howled, but for a brief moment it was as if they stood beneath a glass dome protecting them from the elements and nothing mattered beyond their beating hearts.

For two days, they'd talked, discussed and prepared together, and each moment spent in her company etched itself on Jason's heart. He'd come to enjoy this woman's sharp wit and agile mind. Her loyalty and bravery were admirable traits, but the flashes of vulnerability drew him in. As tough and capable as Angie was, Jason sensed there was a woman inside whose polished exterior longed to be cherished. And against his better judgment, he longed to be the one to cherish her.

The boat bumped against the dock. The reverberation knocked Jason slightly off balance. He reached for Angie's shoulders to steady them both. She blinked. Her lips parted and her eyes beckoned him closer.

He didn't even try to stop the impulse overwhelming him. He dipped his head. She drew in a sharp intake of breath just as his mouth covered hers. She was warm and pliant in his arms. It would be so easy to forget their purpose and just lose himself in the moment.

But the knocking of the port bow against the wooden planks demanded attention and forced him to realize his foolishness. Romance and undercover work didn't mix. Letting himself get caught up in emotions could get them killed.

Pulling free from the kiss, he covered his lapse in self-control by flashing a grin at the disoriented glaze in her eyes.

"Steady now." He eased his hands from her shoulders, ready to catch her if she wobbled.

Her gaze clearing, she stepped back and braced her feet apart. Color rode high on her cheeks. "The rope?"

From beneath the port-side bench, he pulled out a coiled, braided rope and handed it over to her. He then tossed three buoys over the side to buffer the boat against the wood before jumping onto the dock. He caught the rope she flung toward him. Quickly, using a round-turn two-and-a-half-hitched knot, he tied the port bow and the port quarter to the mooring posts.

Angie climbed from the boat without help, carrying the duffel bag they'd stuffed with all the necessary equipment they'd need for a stakeout and surveillance. He relieved her of the burden—grateful, she didn't protest.

In tacit agreement, they headed down the beach to where the cliff jutted out to form a blockade to the cove. Keeping their heads bowed against the rain, they scrambled uphill, climbing over the boulders and through the thick foliage. The ground beneath their feet became slick mud as water sluiced off the leaves in little fountains.

Thorns of several sweet acacia bushes scratched at Jason's pants and rain slicker. He glanced back to check on Angie. She trudged along, with no signs of slowing down. He smiled with satisfaction and admiration. She glanced up just then and smiled back. He felt the impact hit his solar plexus and smash into his spine.

Wow, he really needed to take a reality check. Getting emotionally involved with the pretty detective wasn't something he could allow. He'd tried romance before with disastrous results. He didn't want to hurt Angie.

Unfortunately, he had a feeling he was fighting a losing battle.

They neared the top of the hill and worked their way over the loose terrain of mud, rocks and inkberry plants to the other side of the hill from their boat where they could see into the cove below. Finding a relatively flat spot, he stopped and dropped to his haunches. Angie did the same.

"This looks like a good place," Jason said, his voice carrying on the wind.

Angie nodded, her squinted gaze trained on the cove below.

Knowing they'd have a better view through the lens of binoculars and camera, Jason opened the duffel, shook out a camouflaged tarp and laid it on the ground. Then he handed Angie a pair of high-powered binoculars while he took out his long-lens camera, now wrapped tight in plastic wrap to protect its delicate internal parts from the pelting rain. Lying flat on his stomach, he positioned the lens for best coverage of the bay.

Far below, only one of the Corrindas' boats, the *Courir le Soleil,* was moored at the dock. The cove was a hive of activity as men moved in and around the tunnel carved into the wall opposite Jason and Angie. Off to the side, more men stood beneath a canopy that provided some shelter from the raging storm. Waiting for what? Jason glanced at his watch. Nearly time.

"What's this?" Angie said, tapping his shoulder and indicating seaward.

He swung the lens around to view a large, tri-deck motor yacht setting anchor out in the ocean directly facing the mouth of the cove. Jason let out a low whistle. The vessel reeked of money.

The mammoth boat listed with each wind-whipped swell but rode high enough to gently crest until the next one. Jason snapped off shots hoping to get some markers that could help identify the boat and its owner.

From the leeward side of the large vessel, the Corrindas' other boat, the Bowrider, which had stopped them that first night, sped into view, entered the cove and headed for the dock. Jason continued to snap off photos, but the angle wasn't right, so he couldn't get a clear picture of the occupants. He'd have to wait until the boat moored.

Inside the cove, men scurried to the dock to help bring the Bowrider in. Lines were cast and tied off. Jason snapped off pictures as a tall black man wearing white, loose-fitting pants and a lightweight wind-breaker stepped off the boat onto the dock.

"Do you recognize him?" Angie asked.

Adrenaline pumped through Jason. "No. I'll bet it's Mabuto. His name didn't ring any bells when I entered it into the database, but once I download his picture to Interpol we'll know more."

"Look," Angie exclaimed. "Chief Decker and one of the grandsons."

Jason widened the view on the lens to see two men emerge from the protective structure that connected the cove to the estate and greet Mabuto. There was no mistaking Decker. He wore a long rain slicker over his uniform but no hat to cover his silver hair. The other guy was younger, athletic-looking with a baseball cap pulled low obscuring his face, jeans and a rain coat.

"Decker, what are you up to?" Jason wondered aloud.

With rapt fascination, Jason watched through the lens as he continued to click off photos. The three men moved to the shelter of the canopy. Jason zoomed in for a tighter glimpse. After a moment, Mabuto produced a small pouch from the inside of his windbreaker.

Jason held his breath. He couldn't believe what he was seeing. Mabuto poured out the contents of the pouch into Decker's outstretched hand.

"Are those…?" Angie trailed off, her voice echoing the disbelief and excitement Jason felt in his gut.

"Yeah, they are. Diamonds."

Thousands of dollars' worth of diamonds glittered in Decker's hand despite the cloudy and gray sky. They had to be conflict diamonds, smuggled out of the Congo or Sierra Leone or any number of other war-torn places throughout the continent of Africa. Blood diamonds, as some called them, because of the blood-shed the diamonds funded. Rage boiled in Jason's gut. "A clear violation of the Neutrality Act."

"Hey, hey, that's the bag I saw." Angie's agitated voice brought Jason back to focus.

The Hispanic man, Hector Ramirez, carried the long black bag and laid it at the man's feet. Mabuto bent, unzipped the container and peeled back the sides exposing something tightly shrink-wrapped with plastic. Obviously the wrapper had to be waterproof. Mabuto held out his hand. Ramirez offered him a switchblade. Another man opened an umbrella to cover Mabuto and the bag. With a long swipe, Mabuto cut through the plastic to reveal three long gleaming surface-to-air missiles. Seeming satisfied with the contents, Mabuto rezipped the bag and had it taken to his boat.

Jason's breath caught in his throat as dread swamped him. "Oh, man. We've got to go." He backed away from the edge and tugged on Angie. "Come on. Now." He stuffed the camera back into the duffel. "I've got to call this in and get something going before we lose this opportunity. Once Mabuto gets back on his yacht and out to sea we'll have lost him."

Angie scrambled backward and handed him the

binoculars. "So Decker and the Corrindas are dealing in illegal weapons."

"And blood diamonds." Jason hefted the duffel over his shoulder and started back down the hill.

"Obviously the treasure story is just some sort of cover," Angie said as she scrambled to keep up.

"Where does Picard fit into this?" Frustration at the lack of answers poured through Jason's veins.

"Could there be two gunrunners working out of Loribel?"

"Maybe, but doesn't seem likely." His blood quickened. "Picard must be supplying Decker and the Corrindas with the weapons to resell." If he could get Decker and the Corrindas he'd be that much closer to nabbing Picard.

"How quickly can a raid be organized?"

"Not sure. I—"

Something crashed through the bushes to their right. Had they been found?

Angie froze, her breath coming in little audible gasps. Bracing himself, Jason reached for the gun at his back.

A loud hissing sound raised the hairs on Jason's arms. Panic gripped his gut. He knew that noise.

And a gun wouldn't help with this problem.

From beneath the low-branched, thorny sweet acacia bushes, a big, black, five-foot-long alligator charged forward, spraying mud in all directions. A wide-open mouth revealed sharp, pointy teeth.

Even if he were lucky enough to hit the thing in the

brain—which was directly behind its eyes, beneath tough skin and thick skull bone—the gun blast would bring another kind of predator hunting.

"Go, go. Fast," he urged, gesturing at Angie to move down the hill.

The alligaotr lunged. Jason shoved Angie away as he jumped back. Snapping jaws barely missed his leg. Angie lost her footing and tumbled down the hill on a startled squawk, the noise echoing off the boulders.

The commotion would have alerted the men in the cove to their presence. Not wanting to risk losing the camera and the evidence on it, Jason heaved the duffel into the bushes behind the alligator for retrieval at a later time. The beast hissed and snapped his powerful jaws, but thankfully stayed put.

Backing away, with his attention on the creature, Jason made his way farther down the hill to where Angie huddled behind a boulder. Mud covered her from head to toe and she clutched her ankle as if in pain. She must have twisted it on her descent.

"Can you stand?"

"I don't know." She glanced past him. "Is that thing coming?"

"I don't think so, but we've got to go before Decker and his crew find us." He positioned himself behind her and used his arm to hoist her up.

She tested her ability to stand by putting weight on her foot. A slight wince tightened the corners of her mouth. "Painful, but I can make it."

Thunder rumbled overhead as Jason kept an arm

around her, steadying her as she hobbled the rest of the way down the hill to the sand. Just as they reached the beach, the Corrindas' Bowrider loaded with gun-toting men rounded the jetty of rocks.

Jason's heart stopped. There was no way they'd make it to his boat before the Corrindas' men reached the dock. They were done for. He stopped and gripped Angie by the shoulders. "Listen, whatever happens, you take the first opportunity you can to escape."

Angie's eyes widened as his meaning sank in. She reached for her sidearm. "Call for backup."

"There is no backup who can get here in time. We're on our own." He glanced over his shoulder at the speeding boat slicing through the water. "The best we can hope for is to convince them we don't know anything."

"Yeah, right," she scoffed. "You think they'll believe that?"

"I don't know. But put that away." Fear and anger at his stupidity twisted in his gut. He never should have brought Angie into this mess. He should have forced her to leave the island. Now, because he'd let her worm her way under his skin and into his operation, she was in danger. And he didn't know if he could save her. Or himself.

The boat reached the dock and five men disembarked and charged down the beach toward them.

"Play up your injury," he said to Angie.

It took a second before his words registered and then she collapsed onto the wet sand, grasping her ankle and moaning. Jason knelt beside her.

Sand and rain sprayed as the men halted, surrounding them at gunpoint.

Ramirez glared at them. "What are you doing here?"

"Hey, man, am I glad to see you," Jason said, hoping to throw them off guard by welcoming them. "We were on a nature hike and a big old alligator charged us. She took a spill down the hill."

Several men shifted, their guns swinging outward and their gazes searching the area.

"I don't see any gator," Ramirez said, his dark eyes narrowed with suspicion. "Come on. You can explain what you're doing on private property to the boss."

Jason frowned and feigned confusion. "I thought this was a public picnic area." He pointed to the sign at the dock. "Loribel Parks and Recreation."

"That hill is private property."

"There aren't any signs." Jason pulled a face, letting his drawl deepen, which always made people underestimate his smarts. "There ought to be signage, don't you think? I mean, how's anyone to know? That's just not right."

Angie glanced at him, her gaze both amused and terrified.

Ramirez hesitated for a fraction of a second then shrugged. "Not my problem. Grab them and bring them to the boat. The boss wants them alive."

As Ramirez's men stomped forward. Angie reached for Jason's hand and squeezed seconds before they were ripped apart.

He held her gaze, wishing he could tell her they would be all right, that they'd come through this unscathed. That maybe they had a chance.

He couldn't say anything. But that didn't mean he had to make it easy for Ramirez's men. Five-to-one odds. He'd faced worse.

Using the guy on his right for leverage, Jason kicked the man on his left with his left foot, connecting with the man's knee. The guy released his hold on Jason and buckled, going down hard on the sand. Jason head-butted the guy still holding him. The sound of cracking cartilage was muffled by the man's scream.

Jason charged for the men holding Angie. The guy closest to Jason let go of her to raise his gun, but Jason was quicker. He grabbed the barrel of the assault rifle and gave a twisting yank, while his momentum carried him and the butt of the gun into the guy's face.

Angie let out a strangled growl.

Jason whipped around, ready to attack the other two men. Terror stampeded across his brain.

Ramirez had Angie by the hair, her head yanked back and a gun pressed to her face. Blood gushed from the corner of her mouth. "One more move, and she's dead."

Angie had taken out the other guard—he was bent over in pain—but she hadn't been quick enough to get to Ramirez before he got her. Jason held up his hands in a show of surrender.

His gut clenched. Their fates were out of his control. A prayer for help burst from his soul. The words never left his mouth because he feared his prayer would go unanswered.

A blinding pain exploded in his head as the butt of an assault rifle rammed into his skull.

The world went black.

EIGHT

Angie tried to quell her anger and frustration so she could act submissive as her captor practically threw her onto the boat. She inched closer to the railing, wincing at the throbbing in her ankle and her face, and the deep ache in her heart. Jason lay too far away for her to tend to him. To see if he even breathed. Blood covered the back of his head where the guard had hit him.

She took small satisfaction in seeing the blood and bruises Jason had dished out to the men before Ramirez had put a stop to his frenzied fighting. She'd done her best to bring down the man who'd held her by ramming her elbow into his gut and then back-handing him with her fist. But she'd only managed a few painful steps in Ramirez's direction before he'd punched her in the face and then shoved a gun to her temple.

Her lip hurt and the coppery taste of blood lingered in her mouth. *Please, Lord, let Jason be all right.*

* * *

Awareness came in increments. First the pain. Dark and insidious, attempting to pull him under. He couldn't pinpoint the origin. He fought to reach a conscious state, to open his eyes, to move, but his body wouldn't cooperate.

He was on a boat, that much he could tell.

The smell of the ocean, the feel of the waves beneath the hull, the roar of the motor reverberated through him.

He was lying facedown, his cheek resting on the hard wood of a deck. But not his boat. It didn't sound, smell or feel right.

He focused, trying to remember what had happened.

A woman's face floated through his mind's eye.

Angie.

Memory came flooding in, searing his brain with more pain as he realized he'd failed. He'd vowed to keep her safe and he'd failed to protect her.

Shame and despair washed over him, threatening to overwhelm his senses. There was no use fighting the darkness. He was lost already.

"You just couldn't leave well enough alone, could you, Detective Carlucci?" Decker stated, his unyielding expression holding derision and anger.

Angie twisted slightly to better see the chief, who stood alone inside the doorway of the small boat shed where she and Jason were now tied back-to-back against the structure's middle beam. She couldn't see Jason but she could feel his shoulder blades touching hers. He hadn't made a sound since they'd dragged them in here and bound them together. Her stomach churned with anxiety. How badly had they hurt him? Would there be permanent damage?

A snarky remark about dirty cops rose to tempt Angie's tongue, but she swallowed the words back. It was one thing to verbally spar with the men in her family and another altogether to smart off to the man who held power over her life. And Jason's. Instead, she said as calmly as possible, "I don't know what you mean."

Decker came forward and squatted down next to her. "You should have done as I told you. Now you'll have to disappear for good."

Fear slithered along her spine and tightened her shoulder muscles. "Too many people know I'm here. You'll never get away with killing a police officer."

Decker sneered and grabbed Jason by the hair, yanking his head back. "Two cops, no doubt."

"Hey, I'm no cop," Jason said in a slurred voice.

Concern arced through Angie. Did he have a concussion?

Decker rammed Jason's head against the pole. "Doesn't matter. You'll both be fish food by morning." He left, shutting the door of the shed firmly behind him.

"Jason. Jason, talk to me."

"Hmm?"

"Are you okay?"

"Why's the room spinning? How badly are you hurt?"

"Not as bad as you." Tears gathered at the corners of her eyes. Angie squeezed them tight. "Oh, dear Father in Heaven, please, oh, please help us to get out of this." She wiggled, trying to loosen the ropes. "I promise I won't be so bullheaded and dogged anymore."

A tear slipped down her cheek at the words her father always used. Would she ever see her family again? She squirmed more vigorously.

"I promise to go to church more regularly and to…to join the choir."

More tears streamed from her eyes. Her mother was forever bugging her about joining the church choir, saying Angie had a great voice and she should be using her gift to glorify God. Angie wasn't so sure her voice was as good as her mom professed. But her mom was her mom, and mothers were supposed to think their kids excelled even when they didn't. Right? She missed her mother.

"Stop moving so much. You're tightening the ropes, not to mention you're wasting your breath."

She stilled. The scoffing tone of Jason's words was as jarring as the words themselves. She opened her eyes and turned her head in the direction his voice had come from. "No prayer is ever wasted."

"Yeah, well, bargaining with God is a waste." Bitterness dripped from his words, making her ache for him. "The Big Man upstairs doesn't do deals."

She dropped her chin to her chest. There was truth to his words. "You're right. God doesn't want my childish promises. I can't manipulate Him like that. He only wants my trust and love." More tears spilled from her eyes as calmness entered her soul. "Forgive me, Lord."

Jason gave a scoffing laugh. "God lost my trust when He let Garrett die."

"Why would you blame God for your friend's death? God didn't hold the gun, He didn't pull the trigger."

"But He's supposed to be all powerful! He could have prevented it."

The anguish in Jason's voice brought a fresh wave of tears. Leaning her head back against the thick pole, she looked heavenward for help. *What would You have me say to him, Lord?*

If Decker carried out his threat, these could be the last moments she and Jason had on earth. Her heart grieved to think Jason would die with this barrier of blame and anger between him and God.

How could she make Jason see that the evil in the world wasn't God's choice for humans?

The word *choice* played over in her mind, like a gentle whisper. It all came down to *choice*.

"Did Garrett know the danger when he went into that fight?" she asked in a soft voice.

She felt Jason stir. A long moment of silence followed before she heard a faint, "Yes."

"Why did Garrett, or you, for that matter, go into a

situation where you knew there was a chance you could be killed?"

"It was our job," came his harsh reply.

"Right. Your job. Your choice. You said Garrett was a believer. He chose to live his life for God, while upholding the law. He died in the line of duty and I believe, with everything in me, that Garrett is in Heaven now."

"But why did he have to die?"

The question hung in the air.

"I don't know. I only know that God was with him, just as He is with us now."

"How can you be sure God's here?"

She searched her heart, her mind for an answer. "Because I have peace knowing that I chose to trust and love Him regardless of my circumstances."

"You're a better person than I am."

His words pained her. "No, I'm not. I have my moments of doubt and uncertainty. I'm afraid. And I'm angry. Angry at Decker and his men. Angry at Picard for taking your friend. Angry that I won't be able to tell my family goodbye. But I chose to cling to God rather than push Him away."

She wanted to see Jason, to look him in the eye, but no matter how much she twisted and contorted herself, all she could see was his profile in her peripheral vision.

Urgency bubbled in her soul and drove her words. "Listen to me, Jason. God loves you. He wants you to turn to Him, to open yourself to Him before it's too late."

The thought of Jason not reconnecting his life to God before he died wounded her deeply.

"It's already too late. I've pushed God too far away," Jason replied, his voice resigned.

"No! No, it's never too late—"

The door to the shed burst open and three men filed in.

One of the men had a white bandage over his nose. Angie recognized him as the man with whom Jason had fought earlier. In his hands he held an AK-47. "Don't try anything or I'll blow your brains out," he said.

"Come closer, and I'll fix your nose for you," Jason shot back.

The man moved closer. Angie's breath stalled. Would he fulfill his threat? From the corner of her eye, she saw him raise the butt of the gun and then slam it into the side of Jason's head. She heard a sickening thud, felt Jason rock to the side.

Fear made Angie's mouth go dry. "Jason!"

"Is that the best you can do," Jason said, his voice full of mocking antagonism.

"Shut up!" one of the other men snarled. He worked at untying the rope wrapped around their waists keeping them secured to the beam.

As soon as they were free of the wooden post, Angie was grabbed roughly and dragged out the door into the whipping wind and humid rain. A refreshing relief from the stale air of the storage shed tucked back beside the cliff. Dusk had fallen, turning the shadowed cove into a scary pit straight from some gothic story. She tried to stand but her bound feet slipped and slid in the muddy earth. Her ankle screamed in agony. Jason was also being dragged by another man, but Jason wasn't making it easy. He twisted and squirmed, trying to ram his already-wounded and bleeding head into his captor.

They were taken to the dock where the *Regina Lee* was now moored alongside the *Courir le Soleil*. Decker and one of the Corrinda twins—Edmund, she was pretty sure by the cold look in his eyes—stood waiting along with Mubato.

"See, I told you, nothing to worry about," Decker said, his aged face holding a smirk.

"I will not rest until I know that this business is done," Mabuto stated, his dark eyes on Angie. "There can be no witnesses, Picard."

Angie's shock stole her breath. Decker was Picard? No wonder ICE had such trouble tracking him down. Who'd have thought to look at the police chief of this little out-of-the-way island? Now his actions made so much sense. Were the Loribel Island deputies corrupt, as well? Had Picard poisoned them?

"You!" Jason's shocked shout echoed over the sound of the wind whistling through the cove. He struggled against the hands restraining him, but with his feet and hands tied, he couldn't break free.

Hoping to appeal to someone's—anyone's—sense of self-preservation, Angie yelled, "You'll never get away with this. I'm a Boston homicide detective. People will come looking for me." She zeroed in on the Corrinda twin. "Edmund, you can't let this happen. The authorities will come down on you so hard. Do you want that? Do you want to hurt your grandfather like that?"

"Shut her up before the family hears," Edmund commanded. "Get them out of here. Now!"

So only this twin was in cahoots with Picard. Poor Horatio. She had a feeling this would devastate the elderly man.

Picard waved his hand as if he were swatting away an insect. Fury embedded itself in Angie's belly. She lifted her gaze to the house on the cliff. Maybe someone there would hear her scream and offer help. She hoped so as she let loose with all the rage and fear and regret for all that she hadn't accomplished in her life. Her scream rose on the wind. She prayed the sound carried to Horatio or his wife.

A fist slammed into her gut, effectively cutting off her air and her scream. Pain ricocheted through her body.

She was picked up and flung over the shoulder of a big muscular man. She bucked and wiggled in a vain attempt to get free, but his strong hold on her wouldn't budge.

It took three men to carry a wildly resistant Jason to the *Regina Lee,* where they tossed him inside the cabin. He landed with a thud beneath the small dining table. The man holding Angie unceremoniously dumped her next to Jason. Her body bounced and her head knocked against the padded seat bench. The cabin door was pulled shut and locked.

"We're in luck," Jason said. "I can work with being on my boat."

"What are you talking about?"

He inchwormed his way out from beneath the table and over to the kitchenette. "We still have a fighting chance."

All the despair and resignation to their fate Jason had been feeling evaporated, allowing hope and determination to rush in. The pounding in his head even seemed to abate a tad, making his thinking clearer.

Though he was still reeling from the revelation that Police Chief Decker was Picard. How had he missed that?

He turned so his back was to the vertical set of drawers. His fingers fumbled with the handle of the bottom drawer but he finally managed to grasp the lever and pull. The drawer slid open.

"You think luck put us back on your boat?"

He felt around inside for the box cutter he kept in the drawer. "Yeah, I do."

"It isn't luck that's brought us here. I prayed God would get us out of this situation. He answered my prayer."

"If it makes you feel better to believe that, go ahead," Jason said, not willing to give God the benefit of the doubt.

Why would God want to save him?

Angie, he understood. She was good, all the way through. She believed with a kind of faith Jason couldn't. Or could he?

He tried to ignore the deep yearning clawing its way to the surface. He wouldn't be that naive again.

"It should make you feel better, too. God hasn't abandoned us. He never would. Though how being trapped in here is any better than the shed, I'm not sure."

Jason's found the cutter. Turning his back so she could see his hands, he said, "This is why being here is so much better."

She smiled, her bruised and bloodied face lighting up. "God is indeed good."

Just then the *Regina Lee*'s engine fired up and the boat was in motion.

"Where do you think they're taking us?" Angie asked.

"Not sure. Somewhere they can kill us without it coming back to the Corrindas or Picard," Jason replied as he concentrated on contorting his hands so that the cutter could reach the rope around his wrists. He nicked his wrist instead, the sting of the wound barely registering.

"Can I help?"

He scooted over to her and positioned himself at her back. "I'll put the cutter into your hand. You hold it steady and I'll saw my rope over it."

After a few attempts, he finally managed to pass the cutter into Angie's hands without slicing her in the process. Sliding his hands over the sharp-edged blade until he was sure the rope now rested on the blade, he began to saw, gently at first, testing her ability to hold the cutter. She had a firm hold and he methodically moved his bound wrists up and down over the sharp metal.

"Do you think the other Loribel police officers are part of Picard's operation?" she asked.

"Good question. I hope not. One dirty cop was enough. But the attorney general will have to deal with the local issues."

Ten minutes later, the ropes loosened. Victory was in reach. The *Regina Lee* slowed, the engine halting. The rumble of another boat could be heard. A renewed sense of urgency flushed through Jason. The strong, chemical odor of gasoline invaded the cabin, making his nose and eyes burn.

"Hurry, hurry," Angie urged.

The other boat sped away, leaving the *Regina Lee* to bob in the ocean. Soon black smoke seeped under the edge of the cabin door. Outside the porthole windows flames danced.

Shock threatened to siphon his energy. They'd set the *Regina Lee* on fire.

Jason was sure they planned to make it look like an engine accident.

Angie coughed. The blade slipped and sliced the skin on the meaty part of Jason's thumb. Wet, sticky blood oozed down his hand, providing enough slipperiness that he managed to pull one of his hands out from under the loosened rope. "Yes!"

Quickly, he undid the tie at his feet and then took the box cutter from Angie's hand to sever the rope binding her hands and feet. Once they were free of their bonds, Jason checked the door first by pressing his hand to the wood. Heat seethed into his skin. They couldn't go out that way. He scrambled to the forward edge of the carpeted cabin floor.

"What are you doing?" Angie yelled as she tried to break out the porthole window.

"Leave that. We'll never fit through," Jason said. "From that bottom drawer, grab some glow sticks then help me peel the carpet back. Hurry."

Without further questioning, Angie rushed to help. Together they stripped the carpet back to reveal a compartment in the flooring.

Grasping the metal ring, Jason yanked open the hatch and took a light stick from Angie. He snapped the stick, breaking the seal inside activating the chemicals, which caused the stick to glow. He dropped the stick down into the black, gaping hole. "Get inside."

Angie obeyed without hesitation. Before following, Jason lifted the cushioned seat bench and yanked out a hatchet. He jumped down into the false bottom and closed the lid.

"This is handy," Angie said.

Her face was tinged green from the light stick or from fear, Jason wasn't sure which.

"Yeah, never thought I'd use it. DEA confiscated this boat from some drug dealers in Miami."

"Now what? How do we get out of here?" Panic laced very word.

He held up the hachet. "You never know when one of these will come in handy." He began chopping into the hull. In no time, water began to seep into the cramped space as he broke through the wood. The smell of fire eating away at the *Regina Lee* compelled Jason to work faster. Finally, the hole was big enough for them to slip through. The water was rising fast. If they didn't get out quick, they'd drown.

Grabbing Angie's hand, he gave her a reassuring squeeze. "We're getting out of this. Alive."

"I know."

Her certainty filled him with awe. She was so strong and brave. A woman worth more than all the treasure on the island. How was he ever going to say goodbye to her?

He touched her cheek in a quick caress. "I'll go through first. When you get in the water, I'll be there. You hold on tight to me and we'll swim upward." He frowned. "You can swim with your hurt leg, right?"

"Yes. Let's go already."

Admiring her can-do attitude, Jason saluted. "Yes, ma'am."

After stripping off his shoes and stuffing a light stick into the waistband of his camouflage pants, he slipped through the hole into the churning waters of the Atlantic. The salt water stung his various wounds, reminding him of the aches he'd been ignoring. The heavy material of his clothes weighed him down. He shrugged off the jacket, leaving only his black T-shirt between him and the water.

A moment later, Angie appeared at his side, clutching his arm. He motioned for her to remove her jacket. When she'd relieved herself of the weighty garment, he propelled them away from the boat and upward with powerful kicks.

They broke the surface, gasping for breath. The bonfire that once was the *Regina Lee* lit up the dark night sky. Heat emanated from the flames, the intensity stinging her face.

"Someone will see that and come investigate," Angie said as she treaded water beside him. The wind-whipped waters splashed onto her face. She sputtered, spitting out the salty taste while trying to keep her head as far out of the water as possible.

"Yeah, Decker? Or should I say Picard."

"Let's pray not."

"How about praying for the coast guard?" Jason suggested, not really believing such a prayer would come true.

Yet…she had prayed for a way out and they'd been given one. Had God truly listened and acted? Did God really care?

"Hold my hand," Angie said, reaching for him.

He held on. Their legs bumped and butted against each other beneath the water's surface. He found the contact comforting. They were alive and well for now. But for how long? There was nothing to grab on to, nothing to keep them afloat. They'd soon tire and go under. Jason fought off the very clawing at his thoughts.

"Lord, we thank You for bringing us this far. We could use a little bit more help. Could You send the coast guard? Or anyone with a boat not connected to the Loribel police, Picard or the Corrindas would do. We ask this in Your son's name, Amen."

"Amen," Jason repeated, feeling somehow confident that they would be rescued. But until then, they couldn't just stay there tiring themselves out by treading water. He floated on his back while he searched the sky for the North Star. "Can you pick out the Little Dipper?"

"What? This isn't the time for stargazing."

He chuckled. "If we can locate the North Star, we'll know which direction to swim for land. The North Star is the last star of the handle."

"Oh, okay." She tilted until she floated on her back. "Hmm. There?" She pointed to their right.

"Big Dipper. But the two lowest stars of the cup form a straight line to the North Star, which is…right there." He gestured with his hand as he righted himself, once again treading water. "So if we swim in this direction, keeping the star to our left, we should find Loribel."

"We'll find a boat long before then," Angie said as she returned upright to bob in the water.

"From your lips to God's ears," Jason quipped and started to swim.

Angie matched his strokes. They swam for what

seemed like hours. His legs cramped, his arms felt heavy. He could hear Angie laboring for breath. *Lord, help us!*

Finally, a fast-moving boat with a bright spotlight shining on the water bore down on them. Jason halted and began yelling and waving his arms. Angie followed suit.

As the rapidly approaching boat neared, Jason heard Angie say, "Please, Lord, please let this be help."

NINE

"Help!" Angie's throat hurt from yelling, but she wasn't going to stop. They had to get the fast-approaching boat's attention. She really didn't want to drown.

"Hey, over here!" Jason shouted and waved his arms.

The spotlight on the boat moved over them and then stopped. They'd been seen!

Relief turned Angie's tired arms and legs to jelly; she was exhausted, both physically and mentally. But she forced herself to stay alert. They weren't safe yet. Not until they knew who manned the boat.

The speedboat slowed as it neared. Angie bobbed in the wake. Because the spotlight blinded her, she couldn't make out the faces, only the silhouettes of the three men on the boat.

"Help is here," Jason said and slid an arm around her waist.

"How can you be sure?" she asked, while trying not

to weigh Jason down, but she didn't know how much longer she could tread water.

"Don't you recognize them?" He nodded toward the boat.

Squinting at the men, she shook her head. "No."

The boat's engine turned off. A man's deep voice called out, "Agent Buchett?"

"Angie?" another man's voice yelled.

Angie knew that voice, but it couldn't be. Could it?

"Joey?" she said, her voice now hoarse. Joy and relief and amazement burst in her chest. God had answered their prayer.

"We're here," Jason responded in a loud voice. To Angie, he said, "Come on, just a few more feet. You can do it."

With Jason's arm still around her, she forced her muscles to move forward as they swam to meet the boat. Hands grabbed her and pulled her up out of the water. Then she was engulfed in a bear hug.

The familiar scent of her brother Joey's aftershave made her melt with relief against him. But her gaze sought Jason. He was being cared for by two other men whom she didn't recognize. Then one of the men took the helm. The engine roared to life and the boat glided back the way it came.

"Are you okay?" Joe Carlucci asked, his voice full of anxiety and concern. He wrapped her in a warm blanket. "You had me scared out of my wits."

She nodded against his chest, not willing to let go, finally cocooned in warmth and safety. She hadn't realized just how terrified she'd been, but holding on to her big brother gave her comfort and peace.

A shiver ran the course of her body as the last of her fear left. She lifted her head to ask, "Why are you here? How did you find us?"

"I'll explain everything once we get you on dry land and into warm clothes," Joe replied.

She accepted his answer with patience she normally didn't have. It was enough for now that she and Jason were safe. The ride back to shore didn't seem nearly as long as the ride out. In no time, they were docked.

Jason grabbed her hand. "Let your brother take you to the hospital."

"Where are you going?" She didn't want to leave him.

"My condo to meet my SAC."

"But you're hurt."

He waved away her concern. "I've had worse."

"I'll go home, change and meet you there."

He shook his head and touched her cheek with a tender look in his eyes. "No. You need to see a doctor."

She backed up a step. "Don't coddle me."

His expression firmed to respect. "Fine."

Joey drove Angie to their aunt's cottage in a rented coupe.

Angie couldn't believe the relief she felt getting to shower and change from her soggy outfit into clean, dry clothes. Needing the grounding of her professional attire, she slipped on her pantsuit and

Mary Janes. Though her ankle was tender, she remained steady on her feet. She was an officer of the law and there were bad guys that needed to be brought down.

Since she'd known there wouldn't be reception, she'd left her cell at home before going to the cove with Jason. Now she tucked the compact device into her suit jacket pocket. Unfortunately, Picard had taken her Glock, but not her badge, which she clipped onto her belt. She'd have to report her missing weapon in the morning. She grimaced at the thought. The department chief would not be happy. Every time a firearm reached the hands of criminals, the risk to the public increased.

When she came downstairs, she found Joey standing in front of the slider, staring out at the ocean. His slacks and shirt were damp from the ocean excursion. Love for her big brother surged. "Hey, you okay?"

He turned around, his expression grim. "I should be asking you that."

"I'm good."

His tender, concern-filled gaze touched on the bruises that darkened the skin on her face and the cut on her lip, compliments of Ramirez. "You could have been killed. What were you thinking?"

Touched by the love in his gaze, she held up a hand and said, "Stop. I don't need a lecture."

"You wait until Dad hears about this," Joey warned.

That she *could* wait for. As in *never*. She shuddered. He reached for her hand and gave a squeeze. "I can't tell you how glad I am to see you in one piece."

She squeezed his hand back. "Me, too. Now tell me how you came to be here."

"After we talked, I did some more digging. I discovered that your charter-boat captain wasn't who he said he was and there were rumors of Picard on the island. I tried to reach you, but the house phone just rang and your cell kept going to voice mail."

She grimaced. "Aunt Teresa doesn't have an answering machine. Not much cell service on the island."

"Yeah, well, needless to say I got worried. Badgered Lambert into opening up about Jason and the investigation into the Corrindas. Figured I'd come down here to bring you home. Hadn't expected to rescue you, too," he said ruefully. "I'm just thankful the *Regina Lee* had GPS tracking on board."

Surprise washed through her. She hadn't known that.

Joey ran a hand over his stubbled jaw. "When I saw the boat engulfed in flames…" He blew out a breath. "I'm so glad you're alive."

She heard residual anxiety in his voice and though the idea of him feeling as if he had to coddle her stung, she was grateful he'd heeded that feeling. She slipped her arms around him and hugged him tight. "I'm glad you came."

"Me, too." He eased her back, his expression determined. "Now, let's get you home."

"I'm going to Jason's."

"He's fine. We're leaving."

Not about to let her big brother bully her into going, she held her ground. "Are we taking your rental or mine?"

"Angie."

She held his gaze. They'd played this battle of wills often enough. Sometimes she won, sometimes he did. But she wasn't going to back down.

Shaking his head in resigned exasperation, Joey said, "I'll drive."

Smiling sweetly, she kissed his cheek. "Thank you. For everything."

When they arrived at Jason's condo, Jason opened the door.

From the threshold, she wasn't sure what she saw in his gaze. A mixture of relief, pride and something else she couldn't identify. He had changed out of his wet clothes into jeans and a long-sleeved T-shirt, though his feet were bare and his hair was still damp.

She stared at the bandage on the back of his head, the one over his right eye and the ones around his wrists. All stark reminders of their ordeal. A chill raced up her spine. It could have been so much worse.

The urge to wrap her arms around him, to assure herself they were both all right, gripped her hard. She wasn't sure he'd appreciate the gesture in front of his colleagues, so she settled for touching his arm. "Are you sure you're okay?"

He covered his hand with his, the warmth of his skin sending waves of sensation up her arm. "We're alive."

She held his gaze. Something hot and energetic arced between them, sending her heart galloping and her blood racing. They'd shared a traumatic experience; of course there would be a connection.

They'd also shared a kiss. A single kiss. That didn't, couldn't, mean anything. Right? But she wanted it to. She wanted more, in fact. More of him. More of a chance to see where their relationship could go. Yet, how could she want that when she knew how difficult any sort of emotional attachment would be? His job would always come first; she understood that. But was that something she could accept, knowing she'd never be the priority? She wasn't sure.

She was so confused.

From behind her, Joey cleared his throat.

"You remember my brother," she said as she stepped aside so Joey could enter the condo. "He's ATF."

The two shook hands.

"We've known each other for a while," Jason said.

She drew back slightly. "Really? Do tell."

"We worked a joint task force in New Mexico," Jason explained.

"We tried to bring Picard down then but the slippery fox had known we were coming," Joe said.

Angie's heart squeezed tight. That must have been when Jason's friend lost his life.

A banked sadness entered Jason's gaze. He took her hand and led her to the dining area. "Let me introduce you to my SAC, Theo Lambert."

The man rose, a dark scowl on his handsome face.

Discomfort slithered over Angie's flesh. Clearly the man was displeased by her presence.

The big man nodded at her. "Detective. You've made quite an impression."

Not sure what to think of that, she allowed a small smile of acknowledgment.

Jason gestured for her to take a seat. She sat, aware of him standing beside her, so close his hip touched her shoulder. The contact was at once comforting and thrilling.

She turned her attention to the SAC. "So what now?"

"As we speak, a contingent of agents is gearing up to move on the cove. We've been tracking the Corrindas' activity via satellite since Agent Buchett informed me that he suspected the family of being in cahoots with Picard. When we saw what was going down we began mobilizing. We seized Mubato's yacht before it entered international waters."

"That's a relief." She turned to address Jason. "We need to get your camera."

He nodded.

A phone rang. Lambert pulled his cell from the breast pocket of his ICE-issue jacket, stood and moved into the living room to take the call.

"Jason, thanks for watching out for my little sis," Joey said.

Angie cringed at the way Joe said that, as if she was still a kid needing someone's help.

"Hey, she saved my bacon."

"I hope she wasn't too much trouble."

A strangled noise of protest and anger escaped from Angie. Joe barely spared her a glance.

Jason frowned. "No trouble. In fact, she was instrumental in bringing everything to light. Now we know who Picard is and have a visual ID on him. He won't escape us this time."

"That's good."

Angie frowned, not liking to be talked over and left out of the discussion. "Hey, can someone tell me what the plan is?"

Jason focused his attention on her. "We're going to raid the cove and the Corrinda estate as soon as the team is in place."

"Which they are," Lambert said as he rejoined them. He reached out to shake Joey's hand. "Good to meet you. I hope we don't meet again."

Joey grinned. "Likewise."

Lambert looked at Angie. There was dismissal in his gaze. "Detective, thank you for your help. We appreciate it." He drew Jason away and spoke to him in a low whisper before leaving the condo.

"Time to roll." Jason sat on the couch and put on dry socks and shoes. Glancing at Joe, he said, "You'll make sure she gets home safely?"

"Count on it," Joe replied.

"Hey!" Angie scrambled from her chair. "I'm coming with you."

"No!" Jason and Joey said in tandem.

Angie blinked. Her gaze swung from the unrelenting intensity of Jason to the determined gaze of her brother.

No. No way. She wasn't going to be cut out of the operation now. She held up a hand to each of them. "I'm seeing this through and neither of you are going to stop me."

Joey took her hand. "Your part is done."

Wrenching free, she implored Jason to understand. "Would you be able to walk away? Decker or Picard or whatever his name is…tied me up and tried to kill me. I'm not just going to slink off and not see this through. Surely you can understand."

Pain crossed Jason's face. "I do understand. But this isn't your fight."

Indignation reared. "Yes, it is. He made it my fight. I want to be there when he's taken into custody. I want him to know he didn't beat me—us."

She couldn't let the bad guy think he'd won. Getting the criminals off the streets was her job. It was a part of who she was.

Seeing that he wasn't convinced, she added, "I'll stay out of the way."

His gaze narrowed. "Promise?"

"I won't do anything that will jeopardize the operation."

He gave a slow nod of his head.

Angie's heart sighed with gratefulness and…she swallowed, her mouth suddenly going very dry. What was the emotion rising so fiercely to the surface? She dared not look too closely because acknowledgment would validate the emotions and feeling this way invited risk.

Joe sputtered. "What? No. You can't be serious." He grasped Angie by the shoulders and turned her to face him. "No way. Dad would have my head on a platter if I let you go."

"You're not my keeper, Joe. Neither is Dad," she stated firmly. "I'm a grown woman, a cop. I need to do this. Don't you see that? I have to look this man in the face and show him he didn't win."

Joey closed his eyes for a moment then gave a long-suffering sigh. "I do see that." He opened his eyes and stared her down. "We'll go. But you will not leave my side. Is that clear?"

"Crystal," she said, elated that she'd won the small victory. Behind her, Jason chuckled. She whipped around to face him. "What's so funny?"

He sobered, though mirth lingered in his tender gaze. He touched her cheek with the back of a finger. "Nothing. Let's go."

Feeling branded by his touch, Angie smiled, followed him to the door. "Oh, wait. I'm unarmed. Decker, I mean, Picard took my weapon."

"No worries." Jason disappeared down the hall and returned a moment later with a 9mm Sig Sauer.

The compact weapon fit easily into her suit jacket pocket. "Thanks."

"Hopefully, you won't need it."

She hoped not as well, but she felt better armed and ready.

It was time to roll.

* * *

The hot, humid night had calmed. The eerie kind of stillness that came right before the eye of the storm hit ground.

"What's she doing here?" Lambert asked with a fierce glower as Jason escorted Joe and Angie to the base of operations a mile outside the Corrinda estate.

All around them men prepared to raid the estate. A van sat parked on the side of the road. The back door was wide open, revealing the state-of-the-art communication system inside. Weapons were being doled out, flak vests strapped on, night-vision goggles handed out and the plans being drawn up. The contingent of agents wasn't large. Most were from the Fort Meyers station and had driven over the causeway as soon as Lambert got the go-ahead to take down Picard.

No more letting the man off because of intel he provided. Intel he garnered posing as the island's police chief. Just how many of the island's other officers were corrupt? A full investigation into the Loribel Police Department would be launched.

To his SAC, Jason said in a firm yet not belligerent enough to offend tone, "She's a part of this."

Lambert eyed him a moment before relenting with a grunt and returning his focus to the plan of attack being laid out by another operative.

Glad there wouldn't be push-back on his decision to allow Angie on-site, Jason led her and her brother to the perimeter. "You'll need to stay here."

Angie frowned. "No way. I want to see the look on Picard's face when you confront him."

"Not going to happen, Angie," Jason replied, not surprised at all by her desire. He couldn't wait to see the look on the man's face, either, when he realized his plan to get rid of them had backfired.

Joe put a hand on his sister's arm. "This is as close as you get, little sis. Any closer and you're a liability."

She rolled her eyes. "I'm not a civilian."

Jason admired her spunk and determination. Back at the house, he'd also realized he was coming to care for her in ways that he hadn't expected. And as soon as Picard was captured and in custody, Jason planned on finding out just how deep his feelings for the pretty detective ran. He'd found Picard with her; could he find love with her? Dare he? "Here, Detective Carlucci, you are a civilian. A beautiful, stubborn and gutsy one, but still a civilian."

Her eyes widened at the compliment but she sputtered at the insult. "Then deputize me."

"You know I can't do that." He held a hand. "I'm not trying to coddle you. Right now we have to play by the rules. Believe me, I have no qualms about you having my back. But I'm not calling the shots here."

She did understand. That didn't mean she liked it. She turned to her brother. "Joe, go find someplace else to stand."

"Angie, what are you doing?" Joe said in a near whisper to his sister.

"Just give us a moment," she said. "Please."

Clearly not happy to oblige, Joe gave Jason a hard look full of warning before he walked away. Jason couldn't blame Joe for being protective. Angie was his sister, after all. Jason would be the same with his sister if the situation was reversed.

He met Angie's gaze, hoping she could see how much she'd come to mean to him without him actually having to say it. He wasn't good with the mushy talk. Never had been. It was a lame excuse and he knew it. But he wasn't ready to verbalize his feelings. They were too new, and right now, he needed to stay focused on Picard.

"You'll be careful?" she asked, her voice low and a bit unsteady.

"Oh, yeah. You can count on it. You and I have some unfinished business."

"You think?" she said, with a slight smile curving her lips.

He captured her hand and drew him to him. "Yes, we do."

Her arms slipped around his waist. "I like the sound of that."

Using the tip of his index finger, he lifted her face and slowly lowered his head. She took a sharp intake of breath but didn't pull away. He grinned and claimed her mouth. She kissed him back, sending sensations rocketing through him. He deepened the kiss, savoring the moment and wishing it would never end.

"Move it out!" Lambert bellowed.

Jason broke the kiss. Resting his forehead against

hers as he reined in his self-control. "When this is over."

Angie reached up and captured his face. Her lovely brown eyes were tender, yet held a determined light in their depths that Jason found fascinating. "When this is over," she repeated.

"I've got to go."

She didn't release him. "God will be with you, Jason."

He nodded. "I believe that."

And he did. She'd taught him that God did care and did answer prayers. Maybe not all of them in the way he wanted, but at least some.

"Good." She let go and stepped back. "Now get out of here."

He saluted her and hustled to join the other agents.

Joe leaned close as Jason donned a flak vest.

"That's my baby sister," Joe said, his voice full of warning and question.

"Don't worry. I have no plans to hurt her," Jason assured him.

"She's not a fling kind of gal."

"I know that."

"Do you?" Joe's expression said he doubted it. "Her life is in Boston. You planning on making a move? Plan on leaving ICE?"

"I—" Jason faltered, suddenly very unsure of how to proceed.

He was falling for Angie big-time, but Joe was right. The logistics of a relationship with her were unrealistic. Her life, her career, were settled and in one place. His life, his career, didn't allow for a settled existence. He couldn't leave her in the dark while he went on missions. He couldn't do that to Angie.

Oh, he had no doubt she'd understand, but it wouldn't be fair or noble. In the end, she'd end up hurt and miserable. And would eventually leave him. He'd seen it happen to others, had experienced it himself.

Been there, done that.

He wasn't willing to risk that kind of pain again.

"Don't worry, Joe. Your little sister is safe from me."

TEN

Excited anticipation bubbled inside Angie like water boiling on the stove. She couldn't decide if taking down Decker and the Corrindas had her so keyed up or whether it was the residual effects of Jason's kiss.

And his promise that they had unfinished business. As in finding out what the future held for them?

What did the future hold? She couldn't see it, but that didn't mean anything. She knew that trying to control the future was a fool's endeavor.

But she couldn't control the love growing in her heart for Jason. And that scared her. On the surface she and Jason seemed perfect for each other. He wasn't intimidated or turned off by her career. The exact opposite. And they worked well together, she found him attractive and by the power of his kiss, she was pretty sure he found her attractive. They shared common interests and enjoyed each other's company. Sure, there were some logistics that would need to be worked out, but she didn't see that as a major problem.

The one thing that had her hesitating was his fledgling faith. Could she commit herself to someone who wasn't sure about God?

Joe hustled back. Something in her expression must have caused concern because he asked, "You okay?"

"Sure. I just hate being on the sidelines like this."

Joe slung an arm around her shoulders. "I know, sis. I'm proud of you."

His words pleased her. "Thanks."

"Hey, Carlucci!" Lambert made a "come here" motion with his arm.

Angie snapped to attention.

Beside her Joe chuckled. "I think he means me." He ran over to talk to the man.

"Oh, right." Feeling deflated and useless, Angie watched Joe and Lambert talk. Joe nodded and hurried back to Angie's side.

"Seems Lambert talked with my SAC and they want me in on this," Joe explained, clearly excited by the prospect. "You stay here."

Her mouth twisted in a wry smile. "Like a good little dog."

Joe gave her a quick hug. "It's for your safety."

"Yeah, I'm aware of the refrain." At Joe's hesitation, she waved him on. "Go already. Be a hero."

"Love you," he said and jogged away, obviously eager to enter the fight. He donned a flak vest another agent handed him and then he headed up the Corrinda drive and disappeared from view.

A young man came to stand beside her. "Detective Carlucci, I'm Agent Seavers."

"You pulled the short straw, huh? Have to babysit," Angie said, trying to keeping her voice from betraying how frustrated she was at being left behind. She understood why they allowed Joe to participate. He was a Fed. She wasn't.

Seavers's expression reflected discomfort. "Just doing my job, ma'am."

Angie sighed. "I know."

"We can watch their progress on the com," Seavers said and led her to the back of the van where another agent sat monitoring a green-tinted screen. Several red dots moved like ants across the face of the screen. "The red dots are the agents," the man explained.

After several long moments of just waiting, staying like she'd been told to and watching the agents' dots moving about, Angie's restless, antsy nature couldn't take the inactivity any longer. So she couldn't be in the actual raid, but she could do something to contribute. She could retrieve Jason's camera from the bushes on the hill where he'd thrown it when the alligator had surprised them. But first she had to shake her guard.

"Uh, boys, I'm going to take a walk," she said.

Seavers frowned. "Ma'am, you're to stay put."

"There's a public restroom just down the way," she said, hoping her meaning was clear.

"Oh, okay. I'll escort you."

Angie arched an eyebrow. "I think, Agent Seavers, I'm capable of going to the restroom on my own."

"I'm sure you are, ma'am, but I'll tag along nonetheless," the agent said, his voice firm.

Okay, ditching him wasn't going to be as easy as she'd thought. No way would the by-the-book agent let her do what she intended. She'd have to find away to slip away without notice once she arrived at the public bathroom. She turned on her heels and started walking. Her shadow followed.

The access road to the public picnic area where she and Jason had been captured wasn't too far down the road. She quickly headed in that direction. Once away from the lights of the command post, the darkness made the going more difficult, but she managed to find the path and the restrooms. She stopped a few feet from the building. "Agent, stay here."

"Yes, Detective," he replied.

Though she couldn't see his face, she heard the irritation in his tone. She smiled and headed toward the building and kept right on walking. As she started down the incline that led to the beach, she remembered the alligator that had surprised them. Was the critter still lurking about?

She reached for the compact Sig in her pocket. Would a bullet even hurt an alligator? She took a moment to send up a prayer of protection. "Please, Lord, no alligators. Keep Jason and Joe safe, would You, please."

Continuing on, she picked her way along the path. She kept one hand up in front of her face for protection against intruding branches that scraped her arms and snagged on her suit pants. Finally, she emerged onto the empty stretch of sandy and shelled beach. To her left she heard water lapping at the wooden dock and another noise. She paused to listen. It sounded like wood against wood. A boat tied to the pier? She couldn't see anything in that direction. She debated, check out the boat or go up the hill.

She headed right up the hill.

Thankful for the dry weather, she climbed up the hill, navigating through the shrubs and tall grasses, trying to remember where Jason had tossed the duffel bag while also keeping an eye out for the long scaly beast.

There, under the bush was a big black object.

She felt around at her feet for a loose rock and tossed it into the bush. Nothing moved. Breathing a sigh of relief, she scrambled to pull the bag from under the branches of the thick plant.

The bag was heavier than she'd have thought. But it did hold a sizable camera and two pairs of binoculars. Which gave her an idea.

Setting the bag down, she unzipped it, rummaged around until she had a pair of the high-powered lenses in hand, then scurried up the hill to the vantage point where she and Jason had seen Mubato give Decker the diamonds.

Uncaring that she was getting her clean clothes dirty, she lay on the ground and brought the binoculars to her eyes. Too dark to see much. With what little light she had from the moon, she examined the binoculars. There was a lever on the underside. She flipped it. Ah, night vision. She should have guessed that from the beginning.

Below in the cove, federal agents had several of Corrinda's men grouped together. She didn't see either of the twins or Decker.

The door to the small structure in the corner opened and more agents filed out. Jason and her brother were the last to emerge. She zeroed in on Jason's face. By his frustrated expression she assumed he hadn't found Decker.

A noise not far away sent the fine hairs rising on the back of her neck. The alligator again?

Cautiously she righted herself and swung the binoculars in the direction of the noise.

Not an alligator.

There was no mistaking the shock of silvery hair, almost translucent in the moonlight, on Decker's head as the man appeared over the top of the cliff. He rose, unhooked a rope from a metal anchor embedded into the ground and hurried down the hill. Stunned, she realized he'd climbed the face of the cliff.

How had Decker known he would need an escape route? Was there a mole in ICE or ATF?

Another thought hit her. The boat at the dock.

She had to find a way to alert Jason before Decker, aka Picard, disappeared again. But how?

If she fired off a shot, she'd not only alert Jason but Picard, as well. She checked her cell. The word *roaming* flashed at the top. She dialed Jason's cell and heard the ringing sound then nothing. Checking the phone, she clenched her teeth to see the words *call failed*. So much for alerting Jason. She was on her own.

Keeping hold of the binoculars, she quickly stashed the bag with the other pair and the camera back under a bush. Using the night-vision lens to guide her, she followed Picard. A noise behind her sent alarm slamming through her. She swiveled around just as an arm slid across her throat and tightened, cutting off her airway.

She went limp, hoping she'd slip out of her attacker's grasp. Didn't work. Using her heel, she stomped down hard on her attacker's instep. He grunted, but didn't loosen his hold. She used her nails to peel at the man's arm, but her strength was rapidly depleting as her oxygen-deprived brain started shutting down. She wished she'd fired off that shot because not only was Decker escaping, but she was probably going to be fish food.

As the world dimmed and darkness rushed in, her heart pleaded with God to watch over Jason.

"What do you mean she gave you the slip?" Jason roared at the agent who'd been assigned to make sure Angie stayed safe.

Seavers grimaced, his voice echoed with panic. "She needed to use the facilities. She never came back."

Could she have been taken by one of Picard's minions? Someone from the police department? "Did you see anyone? Hear anything?"

"No. She walked toward the restrooms and that was the last I saw her."

Narrowing his gaze, Jason said, "You didn't actually see her go into the facilities, did you?"

Seavers opened his mouth, halted and then shook his head. "No, sir. I guess I didn't."

"She could have walked right past them." Jason wanted to hit something. But mostly he wanted to find Angie and shake some sense into her. Or kiss her, he couldn't decide which.

How could he protect her if she wouldn't let him? How could she do this? Leave, to who knew where, to do who knew what? Rash, impulsive, reckless…so many adjectives came to mind, but the very real fear that something bad had or would happen to her pushed the anger away. Everything inside clenched with dread. He had to find her.

"Have all agents check in. If they see Detective Carlucci, have them detain her," Jason barked to the communications agent. The guy nodded and did as instructed.

An agitated Joe Carlucci rushed to Jason's side. "We have to find her. Where could she have gone? Is there another place on the island that the Corrindas use? Would she have gone to the police station thinking the police chief would be there?"

Jason realized he probably looked just as frantic as Angie's brother. He forced himself to take a deep breath. He held up a hand. "Whoa, dude. We'll find her."

He ran a hand through his hair, trying to put himself into Angie's shoes. She'd been upset to have been left behind, but she'd seemed to understand. But knowing her, even for a short time, he knew she wasn't one to sit idle while there were bad guys to catch.

He glanced down the road toward the public rest-rooms and the path beyond. Of course. He knew where she'd gone. Apprehension chomped through him. Why hadn't she returned yet? Retrieving his duffel wouldn't take very long.

"Come on. I think I know where she went." Jason grabbed Joe's arm and pulled.

"I'm gonna kill my little sis," Joe muttered as he ran alongside Jason. Agent Seavers and another agent followed closely behind.

Flipping on his high-beam flashlight, Jason led the way through the dark past the restrooms to the path that led to the beach. Once there, he swung the beam of light to and fro. The dock was empty, as was the stretch of beach.

He directed the light on the hill but the beam didn't reach far enough. "This way," he shouted and ran toward the hill to get a better look.

"Wait!" Joe yelled, pointing to the ground. "Look."

There were two pairs of boot prints indented in the sand.

But it was the deep grooves following the prints, like someone had been dragged along the beach all the way to the dock, that made Jason's blood run cold.

Had Angie come down to the beach and was now someone's, namely Picard's, prisoner? Fear and panic threatened to consume Jason. His breathing rough-ened and his chest constricted.

Forcing his thoughts to come to order, he issued commands. "Joe, we need a boat."

"On it," Joe said and pulled out his cell. "No service. I'll be back." He took off at a sprint toward the road.

"Seavers, you and Agent Foster head up that hill. Somewhere up there is a duffel bag with a camera that has evidence against Picard." His gut clenched. Unless Angie had taken it. Or someone else found it and then found her… He forced the terrorizing thought away.

"Yes, sir." The agents hustled up the hill.

Jason followed the grooves in the sand to the dock. A rope lay haphazardly on the wooden planks as if it had hastily been thrown off. Dread splintered through Jason. A horrible certainty filled his belly. Angie had been taken away in a boat by the man responsible for so many deaths already. Jason sent up a prayer that Angie's death wouldn't be added to Picard's long list.

Joe raced back and skidded to a halt on the dock. "Lambert is sending one of the boats over from the cove. They should be here any second." He faced the endless expanse of ocean visible beneath the glow of the moon. "But how do we find Angie out there?"

An image of Angie flashed through his mind. So brave and stubborn and rash. All professional in her pantsuit, her curly mane of hair restrained in a band, her big, rich dark eyes so full of trust and affection when he'd kissed her. And she'd kissed him back, making him yearn for more of her.

More of what could never be.

His heart twisted with love. But loving her wasn't smart. Loving her wasn't realistic. They lived in separate worlds that had somehow collided. He'd done a poor job of staying emotionally detached and now she was paying the price. If he'd only forced her to leave the island, she'd be back home in Boston, safe and doing her job. He'd just have to content himself with loving her from afar.

A thought blistered through him. He hit his forehead with his palm. "The tracking device."

"What?"

"I put a tracking device in her shoe. We can pinpoint her location." He started running from the dock toward the path. "I need to get the GPS receiver from my condo."

There still might be a chance he could save Angie. *Please, Lord, don't let me be too late.*

Sensory consciousness happened rapidly for Angie. Keeping her eyes closed, she allowed her other senses to assess the situation. The smell of musty disuse and decaying brine filled her nostrils. The humid air held no breeze. Some kind of closed room. She was able to distinguish men's voices above the roar of the surf. Her hands were tied behind her back in a now-familiar position. So not a good thing.

Her feet also were bound by a thin nylon rope. Thankfully, there wasn't a gag in her mouth. Obviously, she was somewhere remote enough that Picard didn't worry about her screaming to attract attention. A stab of fear made her stomach muscles clench.

She'd put herself in this precarious position by not

doing as Jason asked. If only she'd stayed put. But then Picard would have escaped. It was up to her to stop him. For Jason, for her brother. And for justice.

She cracked her eyelids open to get a partial visual, enough to ascertain the safety of opening her eyes fully. Daylight filtered in through the dirty windows. She'd been out for a long time. Her stomach cramped with hunger, her head throbbed. Tight muscles screamed in agony.

She concentrated on her surroundings. She was in the dining area of a small house. The hardwood floor beneath her was scarred and badly in need of some care. As were the furnishings. Rotted wooden chairs, a table that looked ready to keel over and cobwebs hanging from the low ceiling. What was this place?

She experimented with her bonds. Tight, but at least she wasn't secured to a beam. Cautiously, she turned her head to the right, searching for an escape as well as ascertaining where her captors were. Through the dust-covered window she could see Picard and his cohort—the one whose nose Jason had busted—were outside the house, standing on the porch and blocking the only exit she could see.

She looked around for anything sharp with which to cut her ties. From her vantage point on the floor, she couldn't see the tabletop. She tried to get her feet under her to stand. And fell sideways for her effort.

She tried using her elbow to push herself upright but failed. Frustrated with herself and the situation, she flopped onto her back and stretched out her legs. She stayed prone for a moment, letting her muscles relax and her anxiety lessen, before she bent her knees and rolled up into a sitting position.

Back to where she started. Well, if she couldn't cut her ties, then she could at least hear what Picard and his man were discussing. She scooted her way toward the door. If she stretched, she could just see over the edge of the window sill.

"It's been an hour! Where's the boat?"

There was no mistaking that voice. Decker. Or Picard or whatever his real name was, sounded agitated, and his fierce scowl confirmed it. As he should be. He should be very worried. He'd kidnapped a law-enforcement officer. For the second time. Only this go around, there was backup. Kind of.

If only there were some way to let Jason know her whereabouts.

"Ramirez said he'd be here. He may have had trouble avoiding the authorities," Picard's cohort replied.

"I've got to get off this island."

"What do we do with the cop?"

Angie's breath stalled.

"We'll kill her when she's no longer needed and dump her body in the ocean or leave it here. I don't care. All I care about are these beauties." He held a small pouch and jingled it. "And of course, getting off this miserable rock."

A tremor of apprehension and dread rocked through Angie. Her fate was out of her control. Only God's mercy and grace would see her through this. "Please, Lord, lead Jason to me."

She prayed for the impossible.

As the telltale signs of dawn streaked the horizon, Jason concentrated on the GPS tracking receiver in his hand, watching the little dot. He didn't want to think about the possibilities that crept in to torment his mind. He could only pray that Picard was holed up somewhere with Angie waiting for an opportunity to escape the island. He had to believe she was alive and that there was still a chance to rescue her. Anything else…well, he just couldn't think about that.

He stood on the deck of a fast-moving shallow-bottom ocean skiff provided by ATF. Beside him, Joe gripped the railing, his tortured and anxious expression echoing the emotions bouncing around inside Jason's heart and mind. A southeasterly wind had whipped up. Water sprayed as the slick vessel sliced through the choppy waves. The dot on the receiver began to flash, indicating they were closing in on Angie's position.

They rounded the southernmost tip of the island. Not much development on this end; only the lone lighthouse with its outbuilding stood ready to warn seafaring vessels of the island's existence. The place looked abandoned and forlorn against the emerging daylight. A perfect place to hide.

Going with his gut instincts, Jason instructed the man at the helm to go farther down the coastline before stopping, for fear of alerting Picard to their presence. When the boat set anchor as close to shore as it could, Jason and Joe jumped out. The water came up to their knees.

"Call in our location," Jason instructed the boat captain, who nodded and pulled out a radio transmitter.

Once they reached the shore, Joe asked, "Which way?"

Consulting the receiver in his hand, Jason pointed to the tall, metal tower with a strong beam of light emitting from the glass-enclosed, circular room at the top. The lighthouse was a good two hundred yards away and sat just inland from the beach surrounded by high, spikey blades of grass and the groundcover of inkberry plants. "He's holding her in that building or the lighthouse."

"Let's do this." Joe ran down the beach toward the lighthouse.

Jason followed. His heart beat wildly as he kept his senses on high alert. A man appeared around the corner of the building. Both Jason and Joe dropped flat, hoping the bushes would provide cover. Jason recognized the bandages strapped across the man's nose. Picard was definitely here. Jason's instincts had been correct.

Picard's henchman appeared to be watching the water as if expecting company. Probably their getaway transport.

They waited until the sentry retraced his steps. Then, in a crouch, they ran to the building, weapons drawn. With Jason in the lead, they inched their way around the back. Jason looked in the first grime-covered window he reached. It looked into a small room that probably had once been the lighthouse keeper's quarters but now housed electrical equipment and other paraphernalia for the updated automated lighthouse. No kerosene lantern, no need for a keeper.

The next window gave them a clear view into the main portion of the building. Angie sat on the floor with her feet and hands bound. She seemed to be talking to someone.

Relief made Jason sag for a moment as he sent up a quick prayer of thanks to God. Now, they had to figure out how to get her out alive. He surprised himself by not really caring about what happened to Picard in the process.

"I'll take out the sentry, you get my sister," Joe instructed.

Not one to argue with a good plan, Jason nodded his agreement. Joe crept along the side of the house and disappeared around the front. Jason went back to the storage room window, pried the screen off with a utility knife, slid the window open and soundlessly climbed inside.

A conversation floated to him from the room next door.

"You'll never be free. The authorities will hunt you down for all the days of your life," Angie said, her tone amazingly calm.

"I've done just fine avoiding the law for nearly thirty years. I have no intention of being taken in now."

Picard's answering voice sent rage pounding inside

Jason's head. Not only was this man responsible for his friend's death but he obviously intended to harm Angie. Over Jason's dead body.

"Jason will find me."

Her confidence in him bolstered his determination.

With his weapon at the ready, he tested each step so as not to make a noise as he made his way to the door and cracked it open.

A short hall led to the central room where Angie waited. He crept forward, then peered around the corner and quickly ducked back out of sight as Picard paced, his heavy boots leaving a trail in the dust covering the floor.

Hoping that Joe had managed to disarm and subdue the outside guard, Jason took a steadying breath before charging into the room, his weapon aimed at Picard's head. "Federal agent. Stop where you are. Hands in the air."

Picard whirled around, his eyes widening. "You! I knew you were some kind of cop."

"Hands in the air," Jason repeated.

"I told you," Angie addressed Picard smugly.

Picard raised his hands.

Keeping his gun aimed at Picard, Jason bent beside Angie. "You okay?"

"Yeah. How did you find me?"

"The tracker in your shoe." With one hand, he used the knife to hack away at the rope binding her wrists.

"Track…?" Her eyes widened in comprehension. "Oh, yeah."

The ropes fell away. She rubbed her wrists for a moment before tackling the tie around her ankles.

Jason rose and faced Picard. "You're done, Picard. And I can't wait to see you behind bars."

Picard snorted. "We'll see."

"Let's go." Jason pushed Picard toward the door. The hinges squeaked as the door opened. They stepped out onto the porch.

"Joe!" Angie exclaimed. She started to rush down the stairs but Jason snagged her arm.

Her brother lay unconscious on the ground at the bottom of the stairs. Standing over him was Ramirez. Several other armed goons aimed their weapons at them.

Picard ripped the gun out of Jason's hand. "Well, well, well. Seems the tide has turned."

Jason's stomach dropped as the gravity of the situation hit him full force. Once again they were out-manned and outgunned. He tugged Angie behind him, offering her the only protection he could. They'd have to kill him first before he'd let them hurt her.

He could only pray reinforcements arrived soon.

ELEVEN

Terror for her brother lanced Angie's already frayed nerves. He was lying so still facedown in the sand. Was he even alive? Tears threatened the backs of her eyes but she refused to give in. Emotions right now would only hinder any chance they had of surviving this ordeal.

She tried to step out from behind Jason, but his strong arm held her firmly in place behind his right shoulder. She appreciated his need to protect her. And when this was over she'd thank him. After she'd broken Ramirez's knee.

"Should we duck for cover?" she said beneath her breath so that only he would hear.

"Not yet," he answered her. To Picard, he said, "So take your men and go."

Picard's feral smile sent shivers of dread running over Angie's flesh. The maniacal gleam in his gray eyes didn't bode well.

"And leave witnesses behind who can identify me?" He shook his head. "I think not." He waved his hand in a dismissive gesture and spoke to Ramirez. "Dispose of them."

"With pleasure," Ramirez answered. "Get them all back in the house. We'll torch the place with them inside."

Ramirez's henchmen rushed to do their master's bidding. Two men grabbed Joe and dragged him toward the stairs, while another vaulted onto the porch and gestured toward the door with the business end of his AK-47. Angie clutched Jason's arm as they slowly backed up, her mind rapidly evaluating their options. She didn't think they could take out the five men without her, Joe or Jason getting hurt.

Shouts filled the air.

Suddenly three armed agents came charging from around the corner of the house. Jason took the opportunity to disarm the surprised gunman by kicking the assault weapon from his hands. Angie rushed to Joe, who'd been dropped halfway up the stairs. Seizing the fallen weapon, Jason leaped from the porch and ran across the dry sand to the beach after Picard, who was lumbering toward the awaiting boat. The other agents worked to subdue and contain the men Picard left behind.

Once she was assured that Joe was alive, Angie grabbed a weapon lying on the ground. Her own need to protect drove her to race after Jason, crashing through the tepid and undulating waves until she was within arm's length of him.

He barely spared her a glance. "Go back!"

"No." She pointed to her right where another motorboat was zipping through the waves toward them. "One of ours?"

"Yes. Picard won't get away now." Jason made a motion with his arms for the federal boat to come to him.

Picard swam the rest of the way to the waiting boat and climbed in, yelling for the man at the helm to take off. The boat's engine revved and shot forward.

Jason splashed through the waves to his waist and shouted a warning. "Stop! Or I'll shoot."

Picard ducked down. A moment later, he jumped to his feet and raised an assault rifle. He opened fire; bullets hit the water, precariously close to Jason.

Angie's breath stalled. Terror that Jason would be hit slammed into her chest. She lunged forward to push Jason aside. A sharp stinging pain ripped through her shoulder and halted her in her tracks. She staggered back. She'd been hit.

Jason returned fire in a spray of bullets. The sound of lead pinged off the body of the boat. Picard dropped out of sight as the boat headed out to sea.

Her hand went over the wound. Blood oozed between her fingers. She kept backing up.

Where was Jason?

Frantically, she searched the water for him. Had he been shot as well and was now under the water, perhaps drowning? "Jason!"

The world around her shifted and swirled as dizziness overtook her. She stumbled in the sand and fought to stay conscious, needing to see if Jason was okay, but the pull of darkness was too strong. She toppled over into the churning waves, the salt water searing her wound and smothering her face, filling her nostrils with water. She fought to right herself, to do something, but there was nothing she could do to ward off unconsciousness.

Jason couldn't let Picard get away. Not now. Not after so many months of searching for him, after all the crimes he'd committed. The man had to be brought in. Feeling as though his opportunity to capture Picard was slipping away, Jason flung the rifle aside and dove into the water, intending to meet the ATF craft and pursue Picard.

He heard Angie cry his name. He paused briefly to look back, hoping she wasn't trying to follow him. She needed to stay on land where it was safe.

He frowned as his mind tried to make sense of what he saw. She wasn't following him; instead, she'd dropped to her knees in the shallow water. Was that blood on her shoulder? His breath seized in his lungs. Oh, no. She'd been shot.

She collapsed sideways, disappearing beneath the rolling waves.

All thoughts of pursuing Picard fled. Only one thought clamored through his mind. He had to save Angie. Fear and love and anguish slammed into his chest, forming a tight cohesive ball. He loved her. With every fiber of his being. He didn't want to lose her. He couldn't survive another death of someone he loved.

He swam back, stroking hard to go as fast as his body could. When his feet touched the sandy bottom, he charged through the roiling water to where he'd seen Angie go under face-first. His heart constricted painfully in his chest. The rough surf battered her limp body.

Quickly, he scooped her up and carried her to dry land. "Get EMT here," he yelled to the agents running toward him.

Joe, holding a bloodied cloth to his temple, jumped up from the stairs and raced to meet Jason. Anguish twisted his already battered face. "Is she…?"

"No," Jason barked, not wanting to even think about finishing Joe's question. Gently, he laid her down. "Angie, come on."

"Let me," Joe said and tried to push Jason away.

Panic and adrenaline revved through Jason. He shoved Joe hard, sending him onto his backside in the sand. "Get help."

Joe scrambled to his feet and began to pray out loud as he ran back toward the lighthouse.

Jason checked her pulse. Weak but there. Bending close, he put his ear to her mouth and watched her chest. She wasn't breathing. She must have inhaled water when she passed out.

Placing one hand on her forehead, he lifted her chin with the fingers of his other hand and titled her head back. Pinching her nose closed, he took a deep breath and then sealed her mouth with his. He pushed air into her lungs. Paused to take a short breath in and then repeated the action several times. He stopped to look and listen. She still wasn't breathing.

"Please, Lord, don't let her die. Save her. Save her now."

He was tempted to try bargaining with God. But that wouldn't help. Angie had made him see that truth. He could only trust that God would answer his prayer as he continued with the rescue breathing. Vaguely, Jason was aware that other agents had rushed out to the AFT boat and taken off after Picard. But Jason's main focus was on Angie.

After several agonizing moments, she coughed and sputtered.

"Thank you, God." Jason nearly collapsed with relief. Quickly, he turned her onto her side, so she wouldn't choke on the water her lungs were trying to expel. When her breathing seemed more stable, he cradled her in his arms, gently rocking her.

This was his fault. He never should have let her in on his operation. He never should have let her get so close. He'd almost lost the woman he loved.

A swelling rage rose, choking him on its bitter bile. This was Picard's doing. Once again, he'd hurt someone Jason loved.

"Sir, we need to check her wound."

Jason blinked blankly at the kind face of the blond young man talking to him. He had on a dark blue uniform and reached for Angie with rubber-glove-encased hands.

The paramedic's words sank in. Jason gently handed her over to his care.

Jason rose. A numbness invaded his being as he watched the paramedic and his partner lift Angie onto a rescue litter and carry her away with Joe right on their heels.

Lambert came charging down the path. "Just got a report that Picard went overboard wearing a dive suit."

Worried sick over Angie, Jason tried to comprehend what his SAC was saying. "He got away?"

"Afraid so."

Pent-up fury pounded at Jason's chest. He turned and walked down to the water's edge to stare at the point on the horizon where Picard disappeared.

For the second time in his life he shouted out a vow. "No matter how long it takes or what it costs, I will bring down Felix Picard!"

This time, though, he knew what the man looked like. His face was tattooed on Jason's brain, like a permanent scar.

No way would Jason let the man who killed his friend and hurt the woman he loved live to see another day.

Angie heard the soft yet irritating beep of a heart monitor. She recognized the noise from when her father had had his heart attack. The sound brought back the horrific memories of that time, the anguish and uncertainty that had so tried to rob her of her faith. But she'd held on, knowing God's will would be done.

Thankfully, her father had lived. And though he had to take it easier than he had, he was doing well.

So why was she hearing that awful noise now?

Taking a moment to assess, she could feel the weight of blankets tucked around her. A mattress under her prone body. The antiseptic smell of a hospital teased her nose.

Her eyelids fluttered, allowing in peeks of light through her lashes. Finally she managed to completely open her eyes. Above her the tiled ceiling didn't look familiar. She turned her head toward the incessant beeping. Pain exploded through her system, stealing her breath.

Realization came crashing in. Recollection quickly followed.

She was in a hospital. She'd been shot. Jason had disappeared in the water.

Panic streaked through her. Where was Jason?

She struggled through the pain. Forced herself to lie still and breathe. She had to find out what happened to Jason. The urgency of the thought pushed the pain to the background.

"Hello?" she croaked, her voice barely audible.

Her throat was so dry. She concentrated on gathering saliva to moisten her vocal cords.

She stilled as a noise grabbed her attention. Just a whisper of friction. A door opening?

"Hello?" Her voice came out a tad stronger.

"You're awake."

Jason.

The deep, familiar and oh, so welcome voice made tears pool in her eyes. He captured her hand in his big, strong, warm ones.

Too choked up to try to speak, she squeezed tight.

He leaned closer, his face coming into view. She drank in the sight of him. The stubble darkening his jaw, the concern in his steel-blue eyes and the dark circles telling her he hadn't rested recently.

She licked her dry lips. "Hi."

He smiled. "Hi, yourself."

She could have sworn there were tears glistening in his eyes. Love for this man filled her heart to near bursting. "What happened? Are you okay?"

"Me?" He looked nonplussed by the question. "Yeah, I am now that you're awake. You gave us all a scare."

That his well-being was tied to hers sent pleasure cascading over her, eclipsing the throbbing in her shoulder. "All?"

"Your family is outside."

Her family. Knowing they were close gave her comfort.

"I know they'll want to come in but I'm going to be selfish and make them wait a moment."

"I'm good with that," she said, thrilled by his words. "So what have I missed? Was Edmund Corrinda arrested? Did Horatio know what his grandson and Picard were doing?"

"Yes, Edmund was taken into custody. Horatio didn't know, or at least pretended not to. He arranged for a defense lawyer for Edmund. The other grandson had already taken off for Europe. We're not sure if he had been involved."

"And the treasure?"

He shrugged. "Other than those few gold coins, there doesn't seem to be anything else. Though Horatio vows he won't stop looking."

"And what of Picard?"

His expression darkened. "Escaped."

"I'm sorry. If I hadn't traipsed out into the water, I wouldn't have been shot and you would have captured him."

He brought her hand to his lips. "Not your fault. And don't worry, I'll find him."

"It will be good to see him behind bars."

Something cold shifted in his gaze. He looked away. "Yeah."

Dread like ice water filled her veins. "Jason. You will bring him in. Alive."

He lifted on shoulder in a noncommittal gesture. "I'll do my best."

She didn't believe him. "If there's a chance of bringing him in alive, you have to."

"The man doesn't deserve mercy." The harsh note in his voice echoed in the room.

A deep ache throbbed in her heart. "Everyone deserves mercy. You can't be his judge and executioner. Your job is to apprehend him."

A frown darkened his face. "You're getting upset. Let's not talk about this."

He tried to disengage his hand from hers. She held on like a lifeline. "No. We have to talk about this. I love you and I don't want you to do something that will destroy you."

His eyes widened in shock. "What?"

"You have to understand that if you go after Picard with the intention of murdering him the consequences will ruin you." She had to make him understand. "If you do this, you jeopardize your career and your freedom."

"You love me?"

Her heart opened, allowing all the vulnerable emotions to surface. "Yes. Yes, I do."

The admission was bittersweet because she didn't know if her love would be enough. "But I can't see a future with a man who says he follows God and then does something that out of line with the faith he professes to."

Tears crested her lashes and ran down her cheeks. She didn't care about them. She cared only that Jason would hear and understand. "Your honor and integrity come from God. Please, don't turn your back on that. Take Picard down the right way. The honest and true way. Let justice prevail."

His expression softened. He tenderly stroked back her hair with his free hand. "You're too idealistic for a cop. I will do what I have to do."

"It's not idealistic to follow God and His word."

He shrugged away her words. "I can't promise you anything. Now or ever."

Her heart shriveled. A sob clawed at the back of her throat. His words sounded so final. So cold. So...wrong. "Jason—"

He put a finger to her lips. "Shh." Then slowly he bent until his lips replaced his finger. The kiss was achingly sweet. A kiss goodbye. A deep, gut-wrenching pain filled her. He didn't love her enough to put his need for revenge aside. He didn't love God enough to hold true to his faith.

He straightened and peeled her fingers from around his hand. A sob broke through as Jason walked out.

She closed her eyes and wept for him and for herself. And for what would never be.

Every step Jason took away from Angie was a struggle. He wanted to turn right back around and rush to her bedside. He still couldn't believe she'd said she loved him. His shoulders sagged. He hadn't told her of his feelings. That he loved her right back. It was better this way. Better not to bind ties together that would only hurt worse when they were severed.

As long as she knew what his intent was and didn't know that he loved her, she'd be able to move on with her life. He could only hope he'd be able to move on with his once this business with Picard was finished.

As Angie's hospital door closed softly behind him, he felt as if his heart had closed, as well.

Forcing his expression into neutral, he faced Angie's worried family. They had embraced him into their fold the moment they'd descended on the Loribel Island Hospital and had allowed him to take a turn visiting her, while they waited for her to awaken.

Mrs. Carlucci's expectant face pleaded with him for good news. Angie took after her beautiful mother.

"She's awake," Jason said.

"Hallelujah," Mr. Carlucci intoned. He was a big man with a hard-edged face that spoke of his years on the force.

Mrs. Carlucci rushed past Jason and entered the room. Her husband hurried after her.

Angie's oldest brother, Anthony, stepped forward, his hand held out. He was tall, almost stately, with an intensity to him that fairly buzzed in the air. "Thank you for all you've done for my sister. We appreciate it."

Jason tried not to wince. She'd been shot because of him. He hadn't taken care of her like he'd vowed he would. He didn't deserve her brother's thanks. "I wish I'd done more."

Anthony's lips curved slightly in a semblance of a smile. "There's no taming Angie. She'd have pursued the truth with or without you. I'm glad you were with her."

Love and regret choked Jason. All he could do was nod. Anthony followed his parents into Angie's room.

Jason stared at the remaining Carlucci. Joe's battered face was a blatant reminder of how bad it could have been. Angie could have died and so could have Joe. Jason had put them both in harm's way. Guilt and remorse lay heavy on his shoulders, burdening him with the need to avenge their injuries.

Joe cocked one eyebrow. "So. Now what?"

Forcing Angie's warnings from his head, Jason said, "I go after Picard and take him out."

"Bring him in, you mean," Joe said, his eyes hard.

Another idealistic Carlucci. "Yeah, right."

Joe inclined his head. "And then?"

And then? Good question. He had only one option. "I go back under. There's more of Picard's ilk out there. Someone needs to bring them down."

"Undercover isn't the only way to bring down the bad guys."

"It's the only way I know."

"Then you need to learn a new way." Joe held out his hand. "Be careful. And stay in touch."

Shaking his hand, Jason said, "I will."

Joe started to walk away, but hesitated. He put his hand on Jason's shoulder. "My sister could do worse than you."

Rearing back, Jason blinked. "Excuse me?"

Removing his hand, Joe grinned. "I'm not an idiot. I saw the way you two looked at each other. The way you've hovered here rather than following Picard. You've got it bad, dude. What are you going to do about it?"

Surprised that Joe saw what Jason had tried so hard to hide, he said, "This from the man who'd warned me not to mess with his sister?"

"I said she wasn't a fling kind of gal. If you're not

interested in forever, then walk away and don't look back. Because us Carluccis, we're forever kind of people."

Longing to have a forever kind of life arced through him. He quickly tamped it down. "I'll remember that."

"You do that." Joe saluted and disappeared inside his sister's room.

Jason's mind reeled. His heart hammered. He did have it bad for Angie. But how could he even contemplate a future with her while Picard ran around loose out there?

He couldn't. Resolve and determination shifted into place. He'd allowed emotion to derail his mission once. Wasn't going to happen again. He couldn't let his feelings for Angie detour him. Picard had to be his focus. After that? Well, he didn't know and couldn't guess.

Because if things went the way Jason hoped, Picard would die a painful and slow death.

And Angie wouldn't want him anymore.

TWELVE

Jason wiped away the sweat dripping down the back of his neck with a cloth. He'd been tracking Picard for nearly three months across Mexico and down into South America. Picard's picture had been blasted through all government agencies in every country where the U.S. had intelligence officers. The search had led Jason here, to this jungle oasis where Picard supposedly was hiding out in a small village that was only accessible by foot.

It was midday and the humidity of the Costa Rican jungle was worse than that of Florida. Or it could just be that the oppressive atmosphere lay trapped close to the ground because the canopy of tall trees with their shiny smooth bark and lush, top-growing branches prevented not only the sun from shining through, but also the circulation of air.

In front of him a local Tico, as the native inhabitants of the South American country were called, led Jason through the lush rain forest toward the place where the gringo with the silver head lived.

Picard.

The very thought of the man burned a hole in Jason's stomach.

The man was serious about hiding. But Jason was even more serious about finding him.

A loud bellow echoed through the tropical rain forest followed closely by ear-piercing screeches. Jason knew the second sound was that of the macaw parrots that dwelled within the lush foliage. But the first sound, the almost hoarse roar of some indigenous animal, sent chills cascading down his spine. He adjusted the rifle hanging over his shoulder into a position for easier access.

"What was that?" Jason asked his guide, Al, who seemed unperturbed by the noise.

Al grinned, flashing his yellow teeth. "Howler monkeys. They live up," he said, pointing skyward to the green fauna overhead.

Jason's gaze searched the intertwining branches, leaves and vines above for signs of animals. "Dangerous?"

Al shrugged. "Not unless you climb trees."

Since he wasn't planning to climb any trees, Jason relaxed. "How much farther?"

"Not far."

For another twenty minutes, Jason concentrated on stepping around the vegetation growing out of the rich soil beneath his booted feet. He carried a knapsack with some supplies such as flares, a canteen and some protein bars. His lightweight, olive-colored cargo pants pulled at his hips because of the weapons and ammunition filling the pockets. He was thankful the matching long-sleeved linen shirt absorbed the moisture from his skin as well as protected his arms from the limbs of the shrubbery and sapling trees that made up the dense forest.

Abruptly, Al held up a hand, halting Jason. In a soft voice, Al said, "Just beyond this grove is the village. I wait here for you."

"Will there be guards?"

Al shook his head. "Not here in this direction. Very few know this way." He held out his hand, obviously ready to be paid. Al's confidence in his current employer's ability to get back out of the village wasn't as great as it was in getting them here.

Jason reached into one of his pockets and brought out a wad of colóns, the paper currency of Costa Rica. He handed some to Al. "If I don't return by nightfall, then I'm not returning."

Stuffing the money into his pockets, Al nodded and moved to sit beneath a tree.

Heart accelerating, Jason moved forward, working his way through the tangle of trees and shrubs. He bent down and pulled apart the pointy branches of a tall fern to see into a huge clearing, the village at its center. The many stumps poking out of the ground left no doubt the space had been man-made. The village consisted of several wooden huts positioned around a central common area with a fire pit in the middle. A long table and two roughly made benches were occupied by five men and six women, all of various nationalities. They appeared to be eating a meal. But Picard wasn't among of them.

Frustration churned in Jason's stomach. Who were these people? What were they doing out in the middle of the jungle? The rough look of the group of men was just the type that Picard liked to employ. He needed to isolate one of Picard's people and ascertain Picard's whereabouts.

One of the women, a tall, willowy blonde wearing worn chinos and a loose-fitting blouse, left the table and walked toward the hut closest to where Jason hid. She disappeared into a door, which faced more toward the forest than the eating area.

Stealthily, he crept forward, darting behind the hut. He paused a moment, listening for signs he'd been spotted. He chanced looking around the edge of the hut. The people at the table still appeared oblivious to his presence. On a deep breath, he slipped around the rim of the round hut and into the open door then quickly crouched into the shadows.

A lantern hung from the ceiling giving off a muted glow. The blonde sat on a three-legged stool apparently ministering to a sick person lying on her side on a wooden framed bed.

Jason crept closer. The sick person turned out to be a woman, who moaned and grew restless on the bed. A thin sheet covered her body and her dark hair was plastered with sweat against her brow.

Surprised, he hesitated. Why was the obviously

feverish woman here in the middle of the jungle and not in a hospital? What was Picard up to that he'd keep this woman here to suffer? Jason didn't want to scare the two into screaming, yet he needed answers.

A shout from outside drew the blonde woman's attention. Jason retreated back into the shadows. He breathed out a sigh of relief when she disappeared out the door without detecting him.

Disregarding the danger of contracting some illness, Jason took advantage of the opportunity and quickly approached the sick woman. He clamped a hand over her mouth. Her dark green eyes widened and she struggled. Sweat darkened her brown hair and beaded on her face.

"Shh. I'm not going to hurt you. I need to find this man," he said and held up the picture he'd been carrying with him for the past three months. It was a shot of Picard, dressed as Decker.

She blinked.

"Is this man here?" Jason asked.

She shook her head.

Not sure whether to believe her, he pressed, "Are you sure? If he's not here, then where is he?"

She said something but it was muffled by his hand.

"I'll remove my hand, but don't scream. I don't want to hurt you," Jason said, knowing he'd never be able to follow through on the threat or keep her from alerting the men outside. Hopefully the threat would gain her compliance. "Promise?"

She nodded. He removed his hand.

"Why do you seek him?" she asked in a very Midwestern, American accent.

He hesitated. Was this Picard's woman? Would she protect him at a cost to herself? Jason hoped not. "He's a bad man who's killed and wounded several people."

"Are you the police?"

He decided to play this straight. "Yes."

She seemed to consider that then said, "He went with my husband to the mine."

"Mine? I don't understand?"

"To the north about a half mile is an open-pit gold mine. This man, he owns it."

Jason shouldn't have been surprised Picard was involved in something so dangerous and illegal. Open-pit mining had been banned in Costa Rica for several years now. The very dangerous and destructive process of heap-leaching, with cyanide liquid being poured over the ore collected and bonding with the gold, which was then separated with another toxic chemical, had destroyed huge portions of land and contaminated water with its waste. Just another example why the man had to be taken down and destroyed.

"You're American," Jason stated. "How long have you been here?"

"Five years. Murphy hired our men to work the pit. There are several other villages like ours situated around the mine."

So Picard was going by another name. Wiley of him. And he'd had this operation going while he was also working other schemes. How very enterprising. "How do I get to the mine?"

"There's a trailhead on the opposite side of camp." She paused and squeezed her eyes tight. Pain etched lines in her pretty face.

"What are you sick with? Why aren't you in a hospital?"

She breathed out and opened her eyes. "It's just a bad bout of food poisoning. Charlotte's a nurse."

Good. Nothing contagious.

She reached to clutch his hand. "Go to the mine. You'll find Murphy there. You better go before Charlotte returns."

"Thank you. You've been a big help." He removed several colóns and pressed them into her hands. "I hope you'll find these useful."

She gave him a wan smile. Jason felt bad leaving her to suffer. *Lord, please let this lady be all right.*

He hurried to the door and peered out. He saw the woman Charlotte near the fire pit, heating a huge pot on a metal grate over dancing flames. These people liked things rustic. In a crouch, Jason darted out the door and back into the thick foliage for cover. He then worked his way around the village through the dense forest, keeping close to the tree trunks for cover. He contemplated going to get Al, but then decided he'd have a better chance of being undetected alone.

He found the trailhead and started up the path. As he neared what he figured to be the half-mile mark, he heard the sounds of machinery and voices.

Finding cover between the curving trunks of two huge trees, Jason watched for several moments, keeping alert for the silver-haired fox that had proved so elusive for so long.

A big, circular pit had been dug in the ground. Various large-scale pieces of equipment such as earth-moving wheel loaders, wheel graders and dump trucks sat around the opening like locusts. A tanker full of gasoline for the equipment was off to the side of the pit. A road had been swathed through the forest for access.

Layered ledges formed a stair-step pattern deep into the earth. He could only see a few men toiling in the tropical sun. The sick woman said there were other villages like hers hidden among the trees. Obviously, it was lunchtime for all the villages.

A flash of movement near the lip of the mine caught Jason's attention.

A man stretched and pulled a wide-brimmed hat from his head revealing his silver hair. Picard.

Victory was so close Jason could taste it. Now he just had to figure out how to get to Picard.

He could just pick off the old weasel right now. The hate that had festered in his soul since he'd held his best friend while he died bubbled up, and Jason lifted the rifle and sighted down the barrel. Picard would be an easy target.

One shot. That's all it would take to rid the world of this man. The rifle was equipped with a silencer. No one would be the wiser.

One shot.

His finger slid against the trigger.

Angie's voice invaded his head. *Take Picard down the right way. The honest and true way. Let justice prevail.*

Jason jerked back, his finger recoiling from the trigger. He shook his head, trying to dispel her words. But his mind refused to release the image of her beautiful eyes staring at him with such honesty and vulnerability as she told him she loved him.

Her words had been a shock. Even now, he had trouble believing she'd actually said she loved him.

But Picard deserved to die. Jason resighted.

Everyone deserves mercy.

He blew out a breath of frustration and anger. And repositioned his finger on the trigger.

You can't be his judge and executioner. Your job is to apprehend him.

A shaky, ominous sensation battered at his heart.

Your honor and integrity come from God.

Was that true? If he pulled this trigger, would he be committing murder in the eyes of God? Could he live with himself? He searched his soul. "Lord, I feel so lost. I miss Garrett so much. I miss Angie," he whispered.

He loved her. More than he'd thought possible. And his faith, a faith so firmly rooted he hadn't even been aware how entrenched it was in him, wouldn't let him kill for the sake of revenge. His faith wasn't just talk. Deep inside he knew that God wanted him to do his job. The right way. With honor and integrity.

He shifted the rifle, sighted for the gas tanker and gently squeezed. The rifle kicked back as a bullet pierced the metal. A stream of flammable fluid spilled on the ground. Jason sighted for the gas tank of the dump truck closer to Picard and squeezed, creating another flammable puddle.

Taking two flares from the knapsack, he lit them and heaved them into the gasoline pools.

Within moments the tank and the truck exploded, the noise rocking the countryside. Men screamed as debris rained down.

Picard dropped to the ground with his hands covering his head. Jason yanked a set of cuffs from one pocket then jumped down from his hiding spot and ran through the chaos, using the dirt cloud as cover, toward Picard.

When he reached him, Jason straddled the man, forced his hands down behind his back and snapped the cuffs in place.

"Hey!"

"Shut up!" Jason countered. Yanking him to his feet, Jason forced a shell-shocked Picard back toward the tree line.

Jason pushed Picard down to the ground behind a pair of curving trunks.

"Not you again!" Picard said, his expression unbelieving.

"Yeah, I'm like a bad penny. I keep showing up."

Picard narrowed his gaze. "My men will kill you."

"Your men are scrambling around trying to figure out what just happened."

From another pocket, Jason retrieved his communication unit. Within minutes, he had his SAC on the line and gave the coordinates of the open-pit gold mine operation, which would be passed on to the country's authorities.

Jason also requested a covert extraction because he needed to get Picard out before the Costa Rican government arrived. If Jason couldn't kill Picard, then Picard was at least going to do some hard jail time in an American prison.

"You did this alone?"

Jason shook his head. "No. I had God on my side."

And the love of a beautiful woman.

"Here you go." Sergeant O'Malley plopped a second stack of file folders onto the desk in front of Angie.

She stared at the pile and then turned her gaze to the older gentleman. "Thanks."

He flashed a grin. "Gotta keep you busy."

"Right." She sighed. For two months now, ever since she'd come back to the station house after a month's leave, half of which was spent recuperating in the hospital, she'd been assigned to desk work for the remainder of her forced light duty, while her partner, Gabe, had been paired up with some rookie.

Granted, she was still having trouble regaining movement back into her shoulder and being relegated to a desk was better than a bed. The bullet had ripped through the tendons and muscles and nicked the bone. Healing and physical therapy had proved to be arduous and painful.

Nowhere near as agonizing as not knowing where Jason was or how he was, though. Was he alive and safe? Had he found Picard? Had he done as he'd said he would do when he found him?

Her heart ached at the thought and she prayed he wouldn't kill Picard, but would instead bring him to justice and let the courts decide his fate.

She sighed. No use spinning those thoughts around again and again. She didn't have answers. Even though she'd tried to find out from various channels, no one would tell her a thing about Jason. *Classified* seemed to be the operative phrase.

Was this a glimpse of what a future with him would be like? Could she handle the not knowing?

Ridiculous questions since there really wasn't a remote chance they'd have a future together. Even if she ever saw him again.

Forcing herself to concentrate, she flipped open the first file and read, making sure all the t's were crossed and the i's dotted.

"Hey, Carlucci!"

Angie glanced up at the sergeant's bellow. "Yes?"

He grinned, his weathered face creasing in wrinkled amusement. "You have a visitor."

She glanced at her watch. Early yet. Her parents usually didn't stop by until close to lunchtime. So who could be dropping in to see her? One of her brothers?

"Send 'em back," she called out and let her attention fall back to the file in front of her.

A moment later, a brush of movement announced

her visitor's presence. She lifted her gaze. A wave of shock blasted through her and she dropped her pen. Jason, looking tan and healthy in chinos and a polo shirt, stood beside her. His handsome face, so dear and loved, held a tender, almost hesitant expression as if he weren't sure of his welcome.

"Hi."

She blinked her momentary stupor away, let out a squeal of delight and scooted back her chair. She jumped up and flung her good arm around his neck. "You're here. You're alive."

His arms closed around her and held her. He nuzzled her neck with a laugh. "Yes, I'm here. Alive and well. But how are you?"

She drew back to stare into his face. "I'm good. Or will be. The doctors say I'll get full use back of my shoulder in time."

His gaze touched on her wounded area and his expression darkened. "I'm so sorry that happened. I should have protected you better."

"Yeah, right." She chuckled. "I was where I wanted to be, doing what I wanted to do. You couldn't have stopped me. And you did protect me and you rescued me, just like a real Prince Charming."

His smile turned wry. "I'm no prince."

She grinned, though it felt forced as she tried to keep her mind from the questions that had been burning her brain for weeks. "But you are charming."

"Some would beg to differ." He sobered and said, "Can we talk somewhere private?"

Heart beating wildly, she took a quick breath. "Sure. Let's take a walk through the park."

She led the way, leaving her work undone and forgotten. As they wound their way through the station to the side entrance, she received encouraging looks from her fellow officers. Her cheeks flamed. Her adventure on Loribel Island had been hot news. There'd been no keeping out the detail of working with Jason. Gabe had teased her that she'd finally found a worthy match.

When they reached the beautiful park that was directly across the street from the police station, he motioned for her to sit on a bench beneath a maple tree. The refreshing early Boston fall air did nothing to ease the mounting tension and curiosity tightening Angie's stomach. She bit her lip, tentative to broach the subject of Picard. And their future.

If Jason had done as he'd wanted to do, she'd be obligated to report it. But then again, he could lie to her and say Picard's death was an accident. And how would she know any different? She hated this untrusting and negative feeling trying to rob her of the joy of seeing him. But years of being a cop had made distrust second nature.

"How long do you have desk duty?"

"Another month," she said.

"I'd imagine that's pretty frustrating for you. You really aren't the type to sit on your hands while there are cases to work."

He knew her so well. "Yes, it is frustrating. But I'll survive."

"Of course you will."

His certainty warmed her.

He took her hand and brought her knuckles to his lips. "I've missed you."

The admission sent ribbons of pleasure curling through her system. She tried to hold them back. She couldn't let herself hope that a future with this man was possible. Not until she had some answers. Taking a deep breath and slowly exhaling, she decided the only way to proceed was straight ahead. "Tell me. Did you find Picard?"

He nodded as he turned her hand over and kissed her palm.

"Is he— Did you— What happened?"

Keeping a hold of her hand, he settled back as he told her of his three-month chase and finally finding him in the jungles of Costa Rica. "Now, he's languishing in prison in Washington, D.C."

A huge sigh of relief melted through her body. She leaned her head against his shoulder. He hadn't killed Picard. He'd chosen the right path. *Thank you, God, for answering my prayers.*

"I'm so glad to hear that. I kept praying for you."

"And I felt your prayers. I'm not going to pretend I wasn't tempted to end his miserable life, but ultimately, I couldn't do it. I want to live a life of faith."

Ecstatic to hear him actually say those words, she said, "I wish I'd been able to go with you. Cornering Picard must have been so gratifying."

Jason snorted. "I'm glad it's over."

She lifted her head and stared into his blue eyes. Chasing Picard had consumed him to the point of obsession. Could he so easily let revenge go? "Really? No regrets for not killing him when you had the chance?"

"No regrets." He shook his head. "You were right. God wouldn't want me to kill out of revenge. There's no honor in that."

Tenderness welled up inside her. "I'm proud of you."

"Thanks." He held her gaze for a long moment. "I'm ready for a change."

"Meaning?" Her heart pumped wildly as scenarios played in her head.

"Meaning no more undercover."

Surprised and yet thrilled, she tugged on her bottom lip with her teeth. Their lifestyles would be more aligned now. But how long would it last? The question dampened some of her enthusiasm. "So then what?"

"I've put in for a job here in the Boston office. I'd be running tactical and supervising missions remotely."

Joy leapfrogged over the doubts worming their way into her mind. "Would that be enough for you? I had the feeling you liked undercover work."

"I do, or did. But I've discovered something more compelling."

She raised an eyebrow. "Oh, do tell."

"I've spent too much time and energy chasing bad

guys and not having a life of my own. I want a life with a woman who will challenge me and keep me on my toes."

Her breath caught and held for a moment. "You think you've find someone like that?"

Tenderness and passion smoldered in his steel-blue eyes. "Yes, if she'll have me."

She smiled coyly as her heart did little flips. "How will she know you're sincere? That you won't take off? Or try to smother her with your concern?"

He reached out to gently cup her face. "I love you, Angie Carlucci. I wouldn't dream of smothering you. I love you just the way you are. Impulsive, rash, brave and smart. And I promise not to leave. Not unless you come with me. And I'm sorry I left for so long without any word. I just had to finish this with Picard before I was free to really live again."

Happiness bubbled inside her, making her giddy. "I love you, too. And I'd gladly follow you anywhere."

He drew her to him. "I'm so glad God brought you into my life," he said right before he claimed her lips.

As she fell into his embrace and savored the sensations ricocheting through her system, her heart agreed.

Thank you, God.

* * * * *

Dear Reader,

Thank you for coming on this adventure to Loribel Island with Angie and Jason. I hope you had as much fun with all the action and suspense as I did writing it. Keeping these two out of trouble was a hard task, but I think they came out better people and found a lasting love.

Though Loribel Island is a fictional place, I loosely based the setting on Sanibel Island, in the Gulf of Mexico just off Florida. In doing my research I discovered there are many buried-treasure legends associated with the island that were fascinating to read about. Also, the beaches sounded absolutely breathtaking. One of these days I hope to visit this island paradise.

Until we meet again, may God bless you and keep you in His care.

Blessings,

QUESTIONS FOR DISCUSSION

1. What made you pick up this book to read? Did it live up to your expectations?

2. Did you think Angie and Jason were realistic characters? Did their romance build believably?

3. Angie had issues with people coddling her, especially her big brothers. Do you have siblings? What is your relationship like?

4. Though Loribel Island was made-up, could you "see" where the story took place?

5. Angie couldn't relax on her vacation. What type of vacationer are you? Do you prefer to be active? Or do you relish sitting on a beach with a good book to read?

6. Though no one would believe her, Angie knew what she saw and pursued the truth regardless of the danger. Have you ever been in a situation where you knew something was true, yet no one would believe you? How did you pursue the truth in the face of opposition?

7. Angie had faith that God would rescue them in their dire time of need. Do you have that kind of faith? Has it ever been tested?

8. Jason felt betrayed by God because of his friend's death. Have you ever felt this way? How did you come to terms with the feeling?

9. Angie wasn't sure she could pursue a relationship with a man whose faith seemed questionable. Have you ever been faced with a situation like this? How did you resolve it?

10. Jason was faced with two choices—take his revenge or follow God's word. Have you ever had to face such a choice? What choice did you make?

11. Did it surprise you to find out that Chief Decker was also Picard?

12. Did you notice the scripture in the beginning of the book? What application does it have to your life?

Here's a sneak preview of
THE RANCHER'S PROMISE by Jillian Hart.
Available in June 2010 from Love Inspired.

"So, are you back to stay?" Justin's deep voice hid any shades of emotion. Was he fishing for information or was he finally about to say "I told you so"?

"I'll probably go back to teaching in Dallas, but things could change. I'll just have to wait and see." The things in life she used to think were so important no longer mattered. Standing on her own two feet, building a life for herself, healing her wounds—that did.

"And this man you married?" he asked. "Did he leave you or did you leave him?"

"He threw me out." She waited for Justin's reaction. Surely a man with that severe a frown on his face was about to take delight in the irony. She'd turned down Justin's love, and her husband of five years had thrown away hers. If she were Justin, she would want her off his land.

"You were nothing but honest with me back then." He leaned against the railing, the wind raking his dark hair, and a different emotion passed across his hard countenance. "I was the one who never listened. I loved you so much, I don't think I could hear anything but what I wanted."

"I loved you, too. I wish I could have been different for you." Helpless, she took another step toward the driveway. She didn't know how to thank him. He could be treating her a lot worse right now, and she would deserve it. "Goodbye, Justin."

"I suppose you need a job?"

"I'll figure out something." Need a job? No, she was frantic for one. How did she tell him the truth?

Find out in THE RANCHER'S PROMISE.
Available June 2010 from Love Inspired.

Love Inspired

Bestselling author

JILLIAN HART

brings you another heartwarming story
from

the GRANGER FAMILY RANCH

Rancher Justin Granger hasn't seen his high school sweetheart
since she rode out of town with his heart. Now she's back, with
sadness in her eyes, seeking a job as his cook and housekeeper.
He agrees but is determined to avoid her…until he discovers
that her big dream has always been him!

The Rancher's Promise

*Available June
wherever books are sold.*

LARGER-PRINT BOOKS!

GET 2 FREE LARGER-PRINT NOVELS PLUS 2 FREE MYSTERY GIFTS

Love Inspired

SUSPENSE
RIVETING INSPIRATIONAL ROMANCE

Larger-print novels are now available...

Love Inspired
SUSPENSE

TITLES AVAILABLE NEXT MONTH

Available June 8, 2010

END GAME
Big Sky Secrets
Roxanne Rustand

RISKY REUNION
Protecting the Witnesses
Lenora Worth

TROUBLED WATERS
Rachelle McCalla

SABOTAGE
Kit Wilkinson